ANDREIA NOBRE

The Grumpy Guide to Motherhood

Necessity is the mother of invention

Copyright © 2022 by Andreia Nobre

All rights reserved. No part of this publication may be reproduced, stored or transmitted in any form or by any means, electronic, mechanical, photocopying, recording, scanning, or otherwise without written permission from the publisher. It is illegal to copy this book, post it to a website, or distribute it by any other means without permission.

Andreia Nobre asserts the moral right to be identified as the author of this work.

Andreia Nobre has no responsibility for the persistence or accuracy of URLs for external or third-party Internet Websites referred to in this publication and does not guarantee that any content on such Websites is, or will remain, accurate or appropriate.

First edition

ISBN: 9798817223552

Cover art by Ivana Moura

This book was professionally typeset on Reedsy. Find out more at reedsy.com

This book is dedicated to all the women who have ever given birth. To my mum, to your mum, to everybody's mum. We are all here because a woman gestated us.

"My mother had handed down respect for the possibilities — and the will to grasp them."

Alice Walker

Contents

Brooding, bro: the stork wish	ii
How to get a bun in the oven	1
Fruitful: pregnant and highly volatile	11
Labour of love	23
Poo talk	35
What about women?	44
Cry baby	59
Your new "nightcap" style	67
Your new flying options	77
Look who's talking	85
The end of the world: in the public eye	93
Any way, shape or form	104
School of life	111
Growing season	123
Mom talk	131
The bottom line	140
Notes	148
About the Author	149
Also by Andreia Nobre	150

Brooding, bro: the stork wish

Brooding. That tingling feeling that many women may feel at some point in their lives. You are an adult human female, and you might be working. You might have a job or a solid career. Or not.

Or you are in a long-term relationship with a man or another woman. Or maybe you're single. Or you have met someone. Or you are getting into your 30s or 40s. And you haven't given birth to a child. One day, this feeling came. The brooding.

You've checked with yourself if you wanted to have children, or if you were ready for motherhood. You have checked your fertility.

You've checked with your partner about children. You've checked with your employers. You've checked other mothers' opinions out. You checked with your mum, your sister, even with an aunt. Or with other female friends, mothers or not.

Or you didn't. Maybe you and a male partner forgot contraception. Or you and him mixed up your menstrual cycle, and now there's a baby coming, and you're not averse to the idea of having a baby, after all. At least you're not averse now. And it was a false alarm, but now you're brooding. You're thinking about it. You checked if that's the right choice right now, or one day.

Brooding can be socialisation, too. After all, women are socialised for motherhood. Girls get dolls to play. Boys used to get them too, a long time ago. These dolls of the past would be wooden dolls, mimicking humans and animals. It would be only later in human's history that childhood, as we know it now, would be created.

> *"Both boys and girls are seen making figures of animals, people, and everyday items from mud, as well as playing with dolls or animal figurines made and given to them by their families."*[1]

It doesn't matter where that brooding feeling comes from, to be fair.

It's safe to say that you are now thinking about getting pregnant and having a child, or an unplanned pregnancy has occurred. Because, make no mistake, the only really effective contraception in existence is not having sex – no other method is 100% effective in preventing a pregnancy.

Pills or vaginal implants can be affected by medication, drinking and health conditions, and fail. If pills are not taken correctly, they can fail. If vaginal implants are not implanted correctly, they can fail.

Condoms can tear. Male partners may use all kinds of lame excuses to not wear a condom, saying things like "there's no sensation". Disclaimer: if you don't want to have children, pinch him, then ask: "Did you feel it?"

Back to contraception fails, though. Even knowing your menstrual cycle very well can fail – after all, ovulation can occur more than once in a month, and if no one told you about that before, how would you know? You can even have been born with "uterus didelphys," which is a condition in which a woman is born with not only one, but with two uteri, and in some cases, this woman can get pregnant with two babies, one in each womb. Sounds terrifying, I know. But that's biology for you.

By the way, it's a rare condition. It can happen, but it's rare.

Or you can have more than one ovulation in the same menstrual cycle. If a fertile woman is on her fertile period, when she is ovulating, having sex with a fertile man can lead to a pregnancy. It's just facts.

Why talk about this in a book about motherhood? Because when a woman can get pregnant, and decides to take a pregnancy to term, she will become a mother. That's why!

In this book, I will navigate in these uncharted seas, for many women, on the path to motherhood. I will also talk about women thinking about adopting a child, a baby, a teenager, at a later point.

I'm going to be talking about women who are mothers, and women who want to be mothers. Even women who didn't want to become mothers, but now are. Buckle up.

Because women will keep having babies, one way or another. Unless humans want to go extinct. So, if that's the case, we might as well have a laugh while mothering.

So, let's get on with getting pregnant – because, after all, many women become mothers because they have gestated a child, and wished to do so. This is a guide to women who have become mothers.

Women who want to get pregnant and become mothers after giving birth, or women who have had children, or women who have adopted a child. Because, why not talk about these women and their reproductive labour? We all are here, after all, because a woman gestated us and gave birth to us, isn't it?

How to get a bun in the oven

Image: Flaticon.com

If you are a woman who became a mother when you adopted a child, look away now. Getting pregnant can be a bloody hard process. Women with infertility issues can tell you all about that. I was one of them. My issue was something that could be easily sorted out: polycystic ovaries. It's a female condition that can make ovulation difficult. In some cases, it could bring a higher level of testosterone to a female body, and that makes it harder for eggs to ripe and be released into the Fallopian tubes to be eventually fertilised. So the eggs do not ripen, or do not ripen properly, they are not released from the ovaries onto the Fallopian tube, and get "stuck" in the ovaries. They may block the passage of other eggs that eventually manage to ripen. And all of the woman's eggs, ripen or otherwise, are stuck in there. Forming "cysts." Well, at least in this condition...

So, let's talk about the basics. What do women who want to gestate need to know about getting pregnant, in the first place?

A female body, with a fertile female reproductive system (with eggs too, no doubt) is a good start. If you have one of those, you need to get the other "ingredient" of the bun you are trying to make. It comes from the other sex, the male. I am talking about sperm, of course.

At this point, women reading this might be thinking that they know what they need to do next in order to get pregnant. Some women might have chosen to get the sperm in an independent way, mind you. Maybe self-insemination. Maybe IVF.

For those of you who are going through the baby making process via intercourse with a man, things might not be all that easy, either. When I was trying to get pregnant for the first time, I didn't know the first thing about getting pregnant, it seems. Well, you know, apart from the fact that having penis in vagina sex can get women pregnant.

Let's talk a bit about how conception occurs, then. To form an embryo in a female body (this is not going to be a biology book, I promise) you need egg and sperm. These two need to meet up, at some point, inside a woman's body. And this is not as easy as it sounds. I'll explain: women normally release one egg per month. Women are born with all the eggs they will ever release throughout their lives, which makes it a very interesting thought: all the eggs that a woman will ever release during her lifetime were already inside of her when she was born.

This means that, when a girl is born, she is born with all the eggs she will eventually release.

That also means that, when a female fetus was developing inside of her mum's uterus, she had all her eggs already in her ovaries. And that also means that our mothers were not only carrying us, girls, but also the eggs that could potentially become our children. Which means that the female "ingredients" for conception of new fetuses have all been inside of their grandmothers. The eggs which produced my two kids have been inside of my mother's uterus before I was born. How awesome is that?

Anyway... back to the basics. Egg and sperm must meet. If you are doing it in a physiological way, there must be intercourse, or penis in vagina sex. But having sex is not a break or make all the time.

You must have intercourse - sex with a male, with vaginal penetration - in order to get pregnant. But this must be in your fertile period! The fertile period is the period in which you are ovulating. Ovulation is the release of the mature egg into the Fallopian tube. But... for the egg to be released, it has to ripen. Eggs that don't ripen are not released. So, a woman must be ovulating while having intercourse, and intercourse must happen when women are ovulating for conception to happen.

Your ovulation period occurs between roughly 10 and 20 days after the start of your menstrual cycle. The start of a woman's menstrual cycle is that first day of full bleeding in your menstruation. "Spotting" - drops of blood, not a blood flow - does not count as the beginning of a menstrual cycle. So, if you mark the first day of full bleeding, you may expect ovulation to occur from day 10. Sometimes, it comes before - that is how women can be caught off guard and may end up pregnant without planning to. What might not be very common is for ovulation to occur from day 20 onwards.

Another interesting fact is that, after the ovulation occurs, your next menstrual cycle will occur, invariably, between 14 and 16 days. If you ovulated on day 10, the next menstrual cycle will come on day 24-26.

That being said, you can see how difficult it can be to actually find that "sweet" slot of time when conditions are just perfect for a woman to conceive and get pregnant.

There are, though, ovulation home tests that you can get to find out when you are ovulating. Or you can use the Billings method - counting the beginning of your menstrual cycle, then observing your mucus around day 10 and on.

It is said that a woman's body temperature can rise a bit around ovulation, and your mucus will become sticky and transparent, like the white of an egg – no irony here – around ovulation.

Other difficulties can come from infertility issues – from both parts, obviously. Of course, living in a patriarchal system, women are checked first whether they are infertile. Not men. Of course they are. Like, the almighty sperm, right? The almighty men. The issue must never be with them, of course not. Are you crazy? (That's a rhetorical question. I know you are not crazy). There are home fertility tests you can buy, too. Or you can have your and your partner's fertility tested in a lab.

Any disruption in the female or the male reproductive system may make conception more difficult.

Egg ripen, egg released, egg reaches the uterus without being fertilised – oh yes, there is that too: the egg is not fertilised while in the uterus. The egg is fertilised only while descending the Fallopian tube.

There are also, surely, the male issues, from a biological point of view: "slow swimmers;" not enough swimmers; erectile dysfunction.

By the way, do you know that the little narrative that the sperm "swims" to the egg to fertilise it, making it as if the sperm is this almighty being, the runner in a marathon, that runs to the egg and the egg just "sits" there, immobile, and waits for it? That's not the whole story! Research says that this is wrong. Although sperm mobility may be an issue to conception, sperm mobility is only half of the story. Even though the egg does not run down the Fallopian tube chasing sperm, sperm does not run all the way up like you were told at school in the biology classes. Yes, the sperm has some mobility, but what actually makes the sperm reach the egg on its way up the Fallopian tube is a vaginal contraction, pushing it up to reach the egg. This vaginal contraction happens with orgasm. Sure, in the last few "miles", the sperm do a bit of a run. But, without the vaginal contraction, it would be very difficult for the sperm to reach the egg.

Besides, eggs can reject sperm. They do, actually, reject them. Otherwise, all human pregnancies would be twins, triplets or more, right?

But, back to the conception possibilities. Once a woman and a man are fertile, a woman is in her fertile period, she ovulates and sperm is trying to reach the egg – what's next?

Does conception just happen, just like that? Well, it's not that simple, sometimes. There will be challenges.

You see, even though is fun for a woman to have sex being on top, that can make conception a bit... difficult. Why am I saying this? Because when I was trying to conceive, I heard all about the "techniques" to conceive when you have a fertility issue. One of them was gravity. Gravity? Yes, gravity. One of these techniques to challenge gravity was to lay down after an ejaculation had occurred. Come on, we are all grownups here. I hope... And I know I said "grownups" instead of adults, but bear with me. That's part of motherhood, too. It's called "baby talk" and we're going to talk about it in another chapter.

Ok, back to conception.

It's not only laying down after intercourse. You would have to lay down for half an hour. And you have to lay down with your legs up. For me, getting pregnant the first time round was not a small deed, I swear to you. I thought I'd bring you this image to make you spill your coffee, if you didn't have to go through something like that.

Oh, and just a little something that can go in this section: remember, a woman can have more than one ovulation in the same menstrual cycle. That means that a woman may release at least two ripened eggs. Isn't that something?

And if each egg was fertilised by a different sperm, this can lead to fraternal twins.

But now, for the sake of this book, let's imagine that everything went the way nature intended for reproduction purposes.

A woman and a man had sex when the woman was on her fertile period, and an egg was released, and the vaginal canal pushed it up, and it reached the Fallopian tube, and the egg didn't rejected it, and a sperm managed to get through the layers of chemicals. And...

> *"The egg does not always agree with a woman's choice of partner,"* research has found.[2]

Yes, that can happen, too. The egg can reject sperm.

But, let's say it doesn't, this time. And so, you finally get pregnant, against all odds.

Unfortunately, things still can go wrong. It is estimated that only 20% of all conceptions will go on and continue through a pregnancy, especially in the first three months after conception.

Also, did you know that a pregnancy is counted from the first day of your last menstrual cycle?

I am saying all this because when I was trying to conceive, I thought that a woman's fertile period was at the last three days of a woman's menstrual cycle. To be precise, the last three days before menstruation started. I am not ashamed to write this. I am furious that I was told that!

So, from now on, the story goes on to the next phase, when a woman gets pregnant. I'll see you in the next chapter: surviving pregnancy!

Fruitful: pregnant and highly volatile

Image: Flaticon.com

If you are a woman who got pregnant, there is a lot to look forward to. That is, of course, if you are a woman who got pregnant for the first time, if your pregnancy is a low risk pregnancy and you wanted to get pregnant. We are going to talk about first babies in this book because, let's face it... having a second or a third and so on - the goddess help us - is almost an entirely different thing. If you have more than one child, you know what I mean. You know that, for your first child, you babyproofed your entire home, but that for you second child, you were just put a gate at the top of the stairs. If you have more, you didn't even put the gate up anymore. You just put some pillows at the bottom of the stairs.

So, assuming you are happy to be pregnant because you are going to have a most wanted child for the first time, or you are having another child - your second, third and so on - let's talk about those months you have ahead of you.

For some women, finding out that they are pregnant can involve a blood test - that's the case in my country, Brazil. For many other women - and their health care providers - an over the counter home pregnancy test will suffice. You can take this test basically anywhere. I advise taking it at home, though. This is where you pee on a stick.

Or you have to collect your urine in a container and then put the stick in the urine in a container. Whatever makes your fancy. That's why I recommend doing it at home, for your privacy. It can spill on the floor, on your hands, on your clothes. It can be messy.

Then, you have to wait for a few minutes to get a result. Most home pregnancy tests will give you two lines if you are "positive." - pregnant. Crossed lines. Or a colour change of some kind. Anyway, you will find out if you are pregnant. All in all, you may have got a positive pregnancy test.

By the way, if someone turns to you and says "Nah, it's probably a "false positive test," tell off those naysayers as soon as you can. I mean, sure, a negative pregnancy test could be a "false negative" test. It can still turn out to be positive if you have tested too soon for the test to work. But there is no such thing as a "false positive" pregnancy test. If it's positive, that's it. Really. Time to celebrate! Some women might want to wait until they announce it, though, because until you are past 12 weeks, a miscarriage is not too uncommon.

My advice, at this point, is to avoid taking a picture of the positive pregnancy test with its two lines.

You can do it, there's nothing wrong with it, really. Apart from the several times that I seen posts on social media with sticks with two lines from women, and was about to congratulate these women on the new arrival, only to find out that those were actually Covid tests, which look rather similar to the many pregnancy tests I took myself when I was trying. So you might want to be careful these days on social media to avoid congratulating women for the baby when they are displaying a picture of their positive Covid tests...

Anyway, now you have to start to prepare for the new arrival. First, antenatal appointments. They can be gruesome, but they can be - literally - life savers. Get your antenatal appointments. In the UK, pregnant women are tested every month for urinary tract infections, on top of a thorough medical history being checked and filed. In Brazil, however, urinary infection is not checked every month most of the time, and is one of the main issues causing premature births in the country.

At this point, we should be talking about those first pregnancy symptoms. Everybody talks about a missing period, but that's not the whole story, many times. Missing a period is a big one, sure. It can even be the case that, by missing a period, you panicked.

Many women, I'm sure, may have spent a large part of their younger years trying to not get pregnant.

Maybe you are one of them, who was caught by a positive pregnancy test by surprise. But, here you are, willing to take this baby to term.

Anyway, there are also other signs that you might be pregnant, which you would like to be on the lookout for.

Tender and/or swollen breasts. Going up one to two trousers sizes for absolutely no apparent reason. A mild, constant period pain. Peeing a lot more. Ungodly and unexplained tiredness and, of course, morning sickness. In my case, I had them all. Plus, my hair falls a lot normally, but it would stop falling during a pregnancy. Also, I got all the premenstrual symptoms you can get during the entire length of my pregnancies. Twice, for nine plus months, it would feel like I was having a long, boring and aggravated PMS.

And morning sickness.

Morning sickness can be mild during a pregnancy. Not all women will get them. Not all women will get them as bad as some of us can get.

Morning sickness is also a misnomer. When it happens, it doesn't happen "only" in the morning. It can happen at any time of the day. It can happen all day long. It happened to me like this. I nearly missed out on a course I was taking. I missed so many classes for being unwell that I ended up missing a bit more than 30% of them, rendering me unable to get my certificate. In some cases, the morning sickness can be so bad that you might end up having to check with your healthcare providers.

Yes, I took a full-time, year round course, studying from 9am to 3am, while pregnant. Pregnancy is not a disease, after all. It's not a medical condition. The difference is that it may require medical assistance, in case it's not a low-risk pregnancy.

Let's focus on that for a bit: pregnancy is never zero-risk. All that healthy women can aspire to is a low-risk pregnancy. And, even then, something can suddenly go wrong, with both external or internal factors coming into place. Stating the obvious, then:

No pregnancy is risk-free. No pregnancy is the same. Pregnancies can not only differ from woman to woman, but they can also differ for the same woman in the next gestation.

But, back to signs and symptoms.

Peeing. Peeing a lot more... now, that's a symptom that may as well affect most women. It can wake you up at night. You can find yourself in urgent need of a toilet in the middle of anything: a work meeting, a movie, a shopping trip - even a short one.

And that's only in the very beginning.

As time goes by, pregnant women can get fluid retention. Yeah, big, swollen feet. Indigestion. Insomnia. Leg cramps. Joint pain. And these are all the "mild ones," if you can call them that. Mood swings. "Nesting instinct?" Sounds about right, despite the word "instinct." Skin changes. Remember that when someone says that you are "glowing" - even though you may feel nothing like that and, in fact, you feel like rubbish. Hair and nail growth - I wonder if someone would find it fun to pretend you are a "witch" now. Varicose veins in the legs. As your tummy grows bigger, stretch marks. Heartburn. Sweet tooth - and consequently, tooth decay.

You might feel quite warm for no reason. Some women might want to put their bra in the fridge for a little while before putting it on.

Some women might have milk discharges from their breasts during pregnancy, way before the baby is out.

If people tell you that you are now "eating for two," ignore them. You are not eating for two. But also, people out there, do not take food away from a pregnant woman. Just, never.

Some crazy people enjoy touching a woman's bump, too. Nasty.

And there may be worse.

Diabetes. You can get gestational diabetes during pregnancy. Even though the symptoms normally disappear after the baby is born, it's still rubbish, isn't it?

Urinary tract infections. Carpal tunnel syndrome. What? And some people wonder why would a woman ever choose to not get pregnant at all. Not you, female reader. You are here. If you are not pregnant, you are thinking about it. You should know what's coming your way. Thank me later!

Haemorrhoids. Piles.

I may add here, at this point, some tips to deal with some of the symptoms described above so that you could possibly have a better experience while pregnant.

Let's talk about the big ones - no pun intended! Here we go:

Tender and/or swollen breasts, sore nipples: you may want to ditch the bras for a while, or adopt more comfortable ones. And loose tops! Breasts can get massive during pregnancy, and they get there very fast in some cases. Take long baths or showers. The warm water may alleviate the discomfort, but take it gently and reduce the water pressure! Also, a policy of no "touchy" might go a long way for pregnant women!

Nausea (let's ditch that "morning sickness" terminology, it's not helpful, me thinks...): eating dry crackers, not staying on an empty stomach - you won't be able to, anyway... - drinking more water. Although, that last one may be quite tricky - because it will increase your urge to pee. And fluid retention. Peeing a lot more is unavoidable, so it's up to you what you choose. Work hazard! Growing a baby is a lot of work.

Tiredness and insomnia: they can get to you very early, too. Power up the "cat naps" whenever you can. Try to not miss your bus stop, train or metro station while you do it, standing up in a crowded transport, if you are using it.

In 2007, I got a badge in the Tube in London, which said "Baby on board." Still, nobody would give up their seats for me.

Backache, especially low-back pain: it will come, but maybe not for all women. When it does, moving your hips around, swaying, might help. A bit of walking, a bit of movement here and there, can also help with fluid retention, nausea, leg cramps (bananas are said to be good for leg cramps, too, and even for indigestion). Unfortunately, it may make you tired. We may never win this battle. This is what we go through. By the way, very soon you will have to start sleeping lying on your left side. Don't ask me why. I have no idea. But it does seem to help with a lot of pregnancy discomforts. I mean, that is, if you get to sleep at all.

Sometimes, I think a pregnancy looks a lot like a game of Kerplunk. You mess with one part, you disrupt the other.

Is there any fun in a pregnancy? Well... some say that women can get more sexually aroused too when they are pregnant. I imagine that this happens to women with low-risk pregnancies, with mostly mild symptoms. As for me, I was too busy embracing the toilet gods to notice.

The most fun I had was, definitely, choosing baby names, packing the baby bag for labour, watching a lot of videos of babies laughing, cute cats or relaxation sounds.

As a side note, it could be useful information to know that some women might only find out that they got pregnant when they go into labour! This is what can happen when women don't have access to regular healthcare or are kept ill-informed about how the female body works.

Another thing is that, even though you may hear a lot about the first, second and third trimesters, pregnancies are usually counted from the moment you missed a period, and in months. And that there are women who may as well only give birth to their babies in the tenth month!

Pregnancy is hard work.

And, if everything goes according to plan, there's labour. Which, as the name says, it's labour. Labouring. It can be hard work. This book is not going to be the definitive guide to all things about pregnancy, however. We've got to cover a lot of more issues about motherhood. Pregnancy, for the women who will have one - or two, or three, or, the goddess of fertility, more - may be only the first step. The next one is Childbirth. It deserves its own chapter.

Labour of love

Image: Freepik.com

Indeed, you must be willing to endure a whole new chapter in your life if you are willing to endure childbirth. There will be women who will go through a normal delivery, and there will be those who will have their babies via c-sections. As many women who became mothers may know at this point, there's been a motherhood kind of war for many years now. You can see mothers debating whether a normal delivery or a c-section is best. Breastfeeding or bottlefeeding. Slings or pushchairs. Disposable nappies versus cloth nappies. Everything is fair game to those almighty women, having their babies. We will see more of these issues later on. But, for now, we will go through the childbirth process.

It might seem a bit unfair to not go through childbirth via c-sections in length in this part, but believe me, this is not an oversight on my part. This is simply because I have no idea what it's like to have a baby through a c-section. I had two normal deliveries. If you ask me about natural birth, home birth, vaginal deliveries with forceps or vacuum extraction, I don't know much about them either. All I know about them is by second-hand experiences from friends and other women. So, bear with me while we go through what it is considered a normal delivery.

In a galaxy far, far away

You may be thinking that I am trying to prank you here. But, in reality, having a normal delivery can feel like that sometimes. As if you are going on a journey to the unknown. Mostly because no one tells you what you might actually experience during one, so you are basically, literally, traveling through uncharted territory. You may want to read a pregnancy guide for that, to help you prepare yourself for labour, to know what to expect.

This may not be enough, though.

In any case, you might read ten different books about labour and still end up not being able to relate to anything that you read in those books. Reality may be very, very different from the theory. Let's cover some basics.

Every labour, like pregnancies and, in fact, like any individual, is unique. A woman might even give birth to two babies or more babies on the same day, and each delivery might be different from one another. Each pregnancy, and each delivery, may lead to very different experiences and outcomes. But there are some things that may remain more or less the same.

Labour can start in many different ways. Even for the same woman. It may start with the break of the waters - when the amniotic sac, the membrane that surrounds the baby, ruptures and the amniotic fluid comes out. Sometimes gushing. It may happen anytime before delivery. It may not even happen - some babies may even be born still inside of the amniotic sac. Some say that, even though that is what the movies say it happens, it's far from being that common, though. It's not the norm, anyway. But, yes, it can happen in this way!

Or it can start with contractions. They might start strong - which is rarer, I must say - or they may start mild and very far apart. See, we are starting to get to that far, far away tone already. The evidence says that contractions that are more than three minutes apart are not, actually, labour contractions, but "pre-labour" contractions. And prelabour can last for days. Or it can last for hours before labour - and active labour - sets in. My first childbirth started with these pre-labour contractions. At 8pm on a Tuesday, to be precise. How were they different from what has happened to me before? Well, at around the second trimestre, 28 weeks in or so, you can get Braxton Hicks contractions. Did you know that? Me neither.

These are contractions, normally pain-free, that "harden" your belly (yes please, more baby talk), in lay terms. More like "tightening," but your entire belly goes hard. If you are reading this while you are experiencing one, go on. Tap on it gently. The entire skin is stretched, isn't it? Like a balloon.

So, my labour contractions started, as I said, at around 8pm on a Tuesday. This is how: my belly would tighten. Mild pain would follow, becoming more painful, reaching a peak of pain, and then the pain would recede, until it went away. And it would not come back for another 20 minutes. These pre-labour contractions may last just about 15 seconds. This is the very reason why it is said that they are not labour - or active labour. But labour contractions, yes, they are like that. What differs is the interval in which they may come, and their duration.

This went on for days. All night long, then through Wednesday, then Thursday, then Friday. Were they all the same this whole time? No, they were not. As pre-labour develops, the contractions start to last longer, and the interval becomes shorter. Contractions will come at shorter intervals, and last longer. And may take you to that galaxy, far, far away, as I said. Because, during the peak of the labour pain, you are not here, nor there.

You might want to concentrate. To deal with the pain in the best way you can.

You might want to shout, to moan, to tell a partner or a birth assistance - like a doula - to eff off and get out of your sight, your way, your life or your face. You may not want to be touched now. You may want to sway, to have a shower, to lie in a bathtub to relieve the pain. Breathe. You might want to breathe. Or your personal space free of disturbance. Space to get through that contraction. You have reached that galaxy far, far away. In Portuguese, we call this place "Partolândia" - something like "The Birth Land." You are there.

In the UK, there's even a thing called "gas and air." That's when you breathe oxygen during labour to help you with your breathing. That's how important it is. Even though, I must say, I had "gas and air" during my first labour, and it was quite the experience. I think I actually got high. At some point, I was using it, while laying down in a bathtub with warm water to help with the pain, and the TV in my room was on. As a immigrant mother, I couldn't quite yet speak English the way I do now. Suddenly, I turned to my husband and asked him why were they speaking in Portuguese on TV. We were in Scotland.

And they were not speaking in Portuguese, of course, they were speaking English, so my husband told me that. I then said: "But I can understand everything they are saying!" That's how high I was.

The thing about contractions is that they eventually stop, even when you are in active birth, when they come every three minutes and may last for a minute to a minute and a half. The reason this is called "active birth" is that, in most cases, these longer contractions, which come at shorter intervals, are actually the ones dilating your cervix. The cervix can dilate until about "ten centimetres/ten fingers." And they will, believe me, you just have to be monitored to check if everything is ok and keep going! Before these contractions, your body is preparing for them.

Another fact about contractions is that, sometimes, they can be really painful. But that painful contraction will never come back. Do you hear me? There will be a point in which they will get painful, even with all the mental preparation you had made previously for them. But, that nasty one? Gone! It will never come back. It's one less contraction until your baby comes. You are one less contraction away from delivery.

My active contractions, on my first labour, only started on a Saturday.

Those were the real ones - even though I was not aware of this at the time. This doesn't have to be the case for every labour. As I said before, every pregnancy and every childbirth experience is unique. But it was the case for me. Some women may have shorter labour than that. My second labour was shorter than that, too. Nine hours of contractions. Active contractions? Probably only about five hours. It is also said that a subsequent pregnancy or labour will be better/shorter than the previous one. It's not always the case, of course, but a woman can only hope.

But another interesting fact about childbirth is that, when everything goes according to plan, this experience can be viewed later as fun. Yes, it may hurt at the time, but it doesn't hurt ALL the time. Contractions do have an interval, where you don't feel pain and can rest a bit. And you better rest. Also, from the moment the baby comes out, all the pain goes away. While the pain is there, however - that's another matter entirely. You may want to punch someone. You may not want anyone touching you. You may want water around your body to cope. You may want to sway the pain away.

The birth of the baby itself is quite... uncomplicated, if you ask me.

Or, at least, it should be. Some women may feel the urge to push, and some may not. It also depends on the way babies are positioned in the uterus. Most babies, to be fair, are head down. Many babies are not. For the babies who are head down, the birth goes like this: the baby "crowns" – the top of their head appears through the vaginal opening. Sometimes, mothers can feel it with their hands. More pushing, for the head to come out. When this happens, the "crown" is on you. You may feel like a Queen. A queen of hearts, to be precise. You are a human with two heads: yours, up, and theirs, down. More pushing, and the baby's shoulders, one by one, comes through. Then, the rest of the baby's body comes through and – you have just given birth! Well done!

Now, at this point, I should say that there are a lot of other things that might happen in childbirth. Contractions, yes. Water breaking, at some point – not necessarily before contractions start. But you may also experience a range of other body functions.

You may fart. You may have nausea. You may even poo. Or have diarrhoea.

You may lose control of most of your natural body functions at the same time, or you may not. I'm mentioning this because we are now entering that part of a mother's life in which, believe it or not, some body functions - yours and the baby's - can become a big part of a woman's life. I'm not only talking about childbirth from this perspective because I went through it, but also because many women also do.

You had your baby. Congratulations! The bonding process may as well start now. Or it can start later. You may want to have your baby placed on your chest, warming him/her up with your own body temperature, and preparing for breastfeeding, if that's what you are up to. You may smile now, if you fancy. There's even a name for this phase: the Golden Hour. It's the first hour after your baby has been born, in which it's recommended that your child is placed on you to establish skin-to-skin contact, make breastfeeding easier to happen, among many other benefits for both mother and baby.

Before we go to the next part, let's talk about another body function: bleeding and placenta expulsion. Because childbirth may be that: guts, gushing, body fluids, pain, strength.

After the baby is born, the placenta has to come out. It normally doesn't hurt much more than the dilation contraction. And it lasts, thankfully, much shorter than the actual birth. There seems to be evidence that breastfeeding may speed up the birth of the placenta. And this first breastfeeding may hurt a bit, too. The science in it is that the suckling of the baby makes your belly contract again. It makes sense to me. Think of those smoothie sachets, like Ella's Kitchen: you can't have the content inside without squishing it out of the sachet, can you? You "squished" your baby out. Now you squish the placenta out.

After the placenta comes out, or after the baby, it's time for the bleeding to start. The bloody bleeding, if you ask me. After a normal delivery, women may bleed for weeks. That's normal. It may not be pleasant, but it's normal. That will eventually stop, too. But your period may be months to come back, because breastfeeding may not prevent a pregnancy, but it may prevent your period to come for a while, especially if you have a regular one.

Also, women who deliver their babies vaginally should be aware that they might keep a big bump after delivery.

That's right: the delivery of the baby and of the placenta does not flatten your belly instantly.

But, when everything goes well, that bump may go away within two weeks to four weeks, just like the bleeding.

Body functions. The female body functions in wonderful ways. But now it's time to head to the next phase, in which your baby is here. Some might say I am being crazy about it. I think that many women can relate to this experience. Let's talk about child rearing - from newborns on.

Poo talk

Image: Flaticon.com

Mother, when you planned – or didn't – to have a baby, you may not have been aware, because no one told you, that a big part of motherhood for some good years may be around... poo. That's right. You heard me. Poo. Not Winnie. The Poo.

Poo during pregnancy – with constipation, with diarrhoea.

Poo during childbirth.

But when your child is born, your life may as well continue to revolve around poo. For starters, in the first ten days of their lives, babies will show a change in their poo colour and consistency. It's a real thing. Your baby's first poo is called meconium. It is said that it's kind of sticky, and green. It may even come out a bit during childbirth – which your health care providers should be aware of, as it can be a sign of baby distress.

Green poop? Yes. The health of your baby can also rely on their poop. It should change in around 48 hours after the baby is born, but it doesn't change overnight. It starts to get yellow. Body functions: you are bleeding, your baby is pooping yellow, sometimes a mustard yellow.

I know what you might be thinking, or maybe I don't. But you may end up with thoughts of a hot dog for some reason. You know, catchup and mustard.

Apparently, there's even a word nowadays for when you research your babies/kids poo for its colour and consistency. It's called "poogle." Parents can go searching for it online – the easiest way, since many have access to the Internet – to check on their children's health.

Anyway, this yellow poo happens more often with breastfed babies. Bottle fed babies may start to have a more brownish poo a little sooner. The nice thing about breastfeeding is that the baby poo is not "smelly." So if you are in this process, you may rejoice on that. At least. Even though it can also be a lot more runny, and a healthy baby will poo for at least four times a day...

And this is one of the reasons that this chapter will talk about poo. Because not only nappies must be changed, but there are a lot of other aspects about poo that not everyone will be aware of.

Nappy changing can be such a... moment. If you had a girl, not only she will poo and pee, but she may also get a vaginal discharge after birth.

Or even a very small "period like" bleeding.

If you had a boy, well... boys are born with penises. Warn to the wise: if you have a boy, watch out when you open a nappy to change it. Boys pee too, of course. Right after you removed the nappy, in fact. And right into your face. Like you see in those boys statues at fountains. Only, your baby is lying down, and no gravity is strong enough – at least on Earth – to prevent the pee from spraying around. You might want to change that nappy quickly to avoid such predicament.

As you go on, nappy changing, breastfeeding or bottle feeding, bleeding and not sleeping a lot, you may also be going out and about. You might be going to the baby clinic to get your baby's weight checked, or out for a cuppa with a friend while your baby is in a sling on your chest, or in a pram. Life doesn't completely stop, after all. Since healthy babies might poo 4 to 5 times a day, and they don't move around that much – babies may start rolling on themselves only around four months – you might also be in for a few times for the dreadful, monstrous, running poo. Because nappies also have their limitations.

The running poo is the master of all poos.

It's the poo that might be a bit more "runny," and since your baby is laying down on his cot or in a pram, and if the nappy is already quite full of pee or previous poo, it will flood that contraption.

Running poo can happen when your baby is lying down. It can happen because the baby has started rolling over. Or because the baby is sitting in a stroller.

The running poo, rushing out of the nappy, will then start covering everything, from bottom to the baby's neck or head. A poo that no amount of baby wipes will be able to get rid of - especially when you're out and about. The only solution is a complete bath. You may feel like the baby's clothes could as well go straight to the litter bin.

And while taking the baby's clothes to wash, if you have managed to suppress the urge to completely discard those poopy baby clothes, you may be covered in poo, too. Please, don't throw yourself in the litter bin. Or throw the baby out with the bathwater.

If you are breastfeeding, it may be less gross than it sounds, because the baby's poo is not very pong. My heart goes out to the mothers and other cares of the bottle fed babies. Hang in there.

But, regardless of a mother breastfeeding or bottle feeding their babies, one thing may be relatable to both: not only you're going to be talking about poo, but you also may find yourself picking up your crawling toddler to smell them. To check for poo. Sometimes, this is the way. Sometimes, this is the only way. If you keep your child's nappy for too long, they may get a rash. They will get a rash anyway, mind you, but it's best to at least feel that you have some control about it. Because you can't avoid talking, smelling or even be covered in poo. Sometimes, you find a brown stain on the top you are wearing and you smell it, in the hope it could be chocolate. Many times, it isn't.

Poo talks may be still in for a while, after those first months. Babies may start weaning after six months – some babies will start sooner, no doubt. Babies may start to sit up too, to eat solids, to smile, to grab things, to stop shaking their heads so much and focus. There may be a lot going on.

They might start taking their first steps at around one year old. And that's a whole other level of poo talk coming your way. Because, even though, in some places, young kids may start potty training at the age of 3 – some even later – in others, kids may be potty training at one or two. They are more mobile, they may be walking with their mothers, fathers or carers to the shops, to the park, to the nursery.

So, with potty training, you still will be talking about poo. Let's cover the basics. Some mothers may buy a cheap, small, plastic pot to take with them on a trip out. Yes, this happens. Me and others mums, walking around, taking public transports, may as well be with our backpacks, filled with nappies, snacks, baby wipes, a toy, a kid's book, a water bottle, a changing mat, nappy rash cream, spare clothes and a plastic pot. Because, sometimes, we won't be able to find a toilet where we are taking the kids out. Or we won't be able to get to the toilet in time. Mothers and other carers might be rushing away to the nearest toilet because you can wait, but your child can't.

Mothers may prefer – or can't – get an extra plastic potty, or a toilet reducer with a step for the big toilet and, instead, have to resort to holding your child on the top of the thing when the time comes to pee or poo. Brace yourselves. It requires muscles of steel. You may end up doing it anyway, regardless, when you come out "unprepared" for shops and other public spaces where there are no other options.

Not only we might be doing this, but we are also talking about it.

We might be taking the kids to a play group, or to a soft play, and we are damn well talking about the poo. That time when your child was making their "poo face" - you know, staring at nothing, sometimes staring at you, with a far-off gaze, or you see that they are "scrunching up" their noses. Or grunting. Or any other troubled expression, followed by a smile of relief. "Grumpy eyebrows," as Magazine Romper described it. By now, with a one or two year old child, you might have learned their poo faces quite well. And you rush to the toilet, and not every time you will be successful.

Another very common situation when you're potty training your child is that they might run away from you around your home when you tell them that it's time to use the potty. They may hide under a table and, when you finally see them, they have a facial expression that looks, at first, as if they are distressed. They turn red! Their little faces look anxious. A bit fixed, paralysed. After a few seconds, they relax and smile at you. Because they just had poo in their nappies... The poo that was supposed to go in the toilet.

We get used to it, in the end. It's just part of what motherhood entails.

We may be well over the teenage years with our children and we're still asking them if they had pooped, or what their poo looked like. After all, it can be very scary to find blood in poo. I got this scare several times. It turned out to have been just a lot of blueberries intake one day.

And then, there are those times when it's you who needs to use the toilet, and you might end up doing it holding up your child with you. Or having a visit from them while you're sitting on the toilet. The endless toilet visits from them, or the times you have to stop, mid-poo, to attend to them.

This might be a good time to talk about some of the other women's needs after childbirth and subsequent months - and years. We deserve it - we made a whole other human being!

What about women?

Image: Freepik.com

For this chapter, I am attempting to revert the infamous phrase that most women have heard, all of their lives, when they were trying to talk about female issues or women's rights. You know the phrase. Whenever women are talking about their lives, their struggles, their needs, there come a bunch of them people of the opposite sex, saying "What about men?"

So... What about women? What about women after giving birth? What happens to their bodies? How are their lives panning out after gestating a new life and giving birth to their bundle of joy? There will be many ways to describe it. It may be easier for some women than for others. Here, we can try to talk about some of the physical and emotional aspects of motherhood.

After a baby is born, the woman who gave birth in a normal delivery may be bleeding from two to three weeks. That may be a bit different to women who had their babies via a c-section.

There's also a difference between women who have normal deliveries or c-sections on the appearance of their baby bumps. I'm told that women who undergo c-sections will have a flatter stomach much faster.

For those women who had their babies in a normal delivery, however - get used to the fact the baby bump may not shrink for a good few weeks. Big, ginormous, flabby chunks of belly on display. It is normal, of course. After all, the skin on the stomach area stretched accordingly to the baby's growth. It won't stay forever, but it does look like a deflated balloon. Don't be defeated by it. Think of it as the end of a party. Well, maybe this is not the best example, though. In a patriarchal society, the end of a party for a woman might be a lot of cleaning up. Accurate in this case too, but still...

On the other hand, women who have had a c-section have told me that, due to the stitches, they were forbidden from talking from 24 to 48 hours after the surgery. They told me that, if they talked, that would open up the stitches.

So there we have it, ladies: either we are left with a deflated balloon stomach while having a period-like bleeding for a quarternight, but not having to endure post-surgery recovery - or at least a few days with a symbolic scold-bridle and stitches to recover from while looking after a newborn baby. Anyway, both mum and baby are now wearing nappies - or equivalents.

Also, stretchmarks. The "baby weight," which might remain for some time – or a long time.

Is that all we might expect postpartum?

Well, that might depend on other aspects of motherhood, of course. Women who are bottle feeding their babies may be exhausted from waking up two or three times every night to prepare the bottle. Mothers breastfeeding might not get it that easier, either. I mean, sure, mothers who are breastfeeding AND co-sleeping with their babies might just pull a breast out and catch up on some well-deserved rest, like I did. But in my case, my younger child breastfed for such a long period of time, I developed a bed rash on both of my hips. Charming.

Another fact that ought to be here is that the very first breastfeeding can have benefits for both baby AND mother. Not only the baby will get colostrum, a fat rich liquid, full of goodies for their immune system, but also these first feedings may help the placenta to come out faster and may help to speed the shrinking of the deflated balloon effect on your stomach. Even though the very first feedings may cause pain as well, mind you. But that's because the suckling will help the shrinking by making the uterus contract.

But of course, there are still the many other issues that can also come with breastfeeding itself, such as mastitis, sore breasts and chipped nipples.

These are some of the worst that can happen, apart from all the leaking that a woman can experience any time, anywhere, day and night.

We shall leak on the beaches, on the landing grounds, we shall leak in the fields and in the streets, we shall leak in the hills.

Sometimes, the baby will cry and the mother will leak breast milk, even if the baby does not necessarily need a feed. Or a woman might leak breastmilk because she thought of her child.

A woman who is a mother might be pumping breastmilk at work.

And the thirstiness. The thirst we experience during breastfeeding itself. The thirst can be quite overwhelming. If you see a mother breastfeeding, and if she doesn't seem to have water around her, offer her some water, that's my advice. I wouldn't even sit or lay down to breastfeed before grabbing a bottle of water to drink. Sometimes it felt like I had been walking for hours in a desert.

And I had my two children in Scotland - a place where stand-up comedians mock the fact that there's a newspaper called "The Sun" - because Scotland rarely sees it. Once I saw a comedian say that when Noah announced that there would be 40 days and 40 nights of rain, and Scottish people laughed and said they were already on 60 days of rain, so jog on, Noah.

Thirsty. Hungry, too. With a sore arm, many times. You might want to consider a support under your baby to relief that.

This shall pass, though, but other issues may arrive.

How lovely it is to see that the baby is now grabbing things. And the baby might grab an earring and pull it. Oh, the baby is getting ready to be weaned off, with teeth coming through? They may start biting the nipple during breastfeeding and pulling it away. Or the biting and pulling may happen because the baby is using bottles or dummies. Watch out for baby bites!

Breastfeeding on demand may mean pulling a breast out when in public in cold temperatures, if you live in a cold place, like I did.

My solution was bras that I could just drop down, combined with tops that could be easily pulled down as well in the same way, to expose JUST one breast - and nothing else. Everything else covered up, protected from the cold.

Oh, and of course, there may be another kind of leaking you may experience as well. That can happen when you cough, sneeze, laugh hard, run or jump. That's when the pelvic floor muscles aren't strong enough to support your bladder, which may or not happen during a pregnancy. Expert Elaine Miller, a Scottish physiotherapist who self-describes as "passionate about pelvic floors" and spends many of her clinic days "elbow deep in leaky ladies," wrote a whole comedy routine on the subject, called Gusset Grippers. According to her, she is a "recovery incontinent" and, after having "three big-headed babies," she became fascinated in sorting out the issue. Miller says that this issue has a solution - only, many women don't know it yet. So she tries to raise awareness of the options available, and encourage women - including mothers - to seek help and get their quality of life back after giving birth.

Apart from all this leaky talk, we may still be recovering from other things as well, like pregnancy brain fog, which can last for a few weeks.

Or we may experience "baby blues," or worse, post-natal depression.

Or motherhood loneliness, which can affect most new mums, because many will experience being seen as a different kind of woman. A woman who is now a mother.

Women who give birth and become mothers are often quite isolated from the rest of the world, once the baby is born. Sometimes, this may be because friends do not contact them anymore, because they can't now go out at night to pubs or nightclubs, or even for dinner at a restaurant.

They can't?!? They can, of course they do. But one thing is being childless and going out with friends. Going out with friends after having a baby is not the same thing. Mothers have to arrange childcare, sometimes pump milk before leaving, there is a whole set of stuff they need to do before even starting to get ready to go out. And they might be wearing breast pads while talking to others, to try and avoid them being "upset" or "disgusted" because they leaked breastmilk.

Other types of motherhood loneliness may come from the rest of society at large.

Like events that don't allow women to take their newborn babies with them. Places where there's no form of childcare, like a nursery, for the babies, notoriously hard to find in universities or workplaces.

For instance, when I had my children, the two cities I lived in - Edinburgh and Glasgow, respectively - had weekly morning sessions at local cinemas for mothers. The sound was less loud than it usually is in other cinema sessions. We could go there WITH the babies, take the baby prams INSIDE the cinema room and watch "normal" movies, not only children's animations. Crying babies were not an issue. It was, in a sense, a way to allow new mothers to do things like that again, without judgment. But how many other places will have a baby-friendly option like this?

The worst kinds of motherhood loneliness may come from the world we live in, where women who become pregnant may lose their jobs, or may not be hired for being pregnant, or may not even be hired for the off-chance that they may want to become pregnant one day.

The women who may be fired during maternity leave, or may be denied maternity leave, or may be fired when they return to work.

The women who may be denied time to breastfeed on returning to work, or who will have to spend most of their money paying for childcare.

The women who are mothers and migrated to other countries. Who face bureaucracy to register as residents, especially if they do not yet speak the local language and, therefore, can't get the help they need, like register with a doctor, get child benefit, or even apply for jobs or housing.

The mothers, native, resident or migrant, who are unable to get help to leave an abusive relationship and have nowhere to go. The mothers who may resort to any sort of self-employment, like selling services without a contract. The mothers who are vulnerable to poverty.

I find that many women start looking up feminism right after they have become mothers. Maybe not like right after their first child - it may still look like such a bliss and blessing for a woman with their first little one bundle of joy. But, oh boy, do women find it that they may go crazy after a second or a third child. And it's not only for baby stuff. After all, all children are different - what may have worked with one child may not work with the next one.

It can start to be only for laughter and bonding between women. I found it so uplifting going to the baby clinic in Scotland and meeting other mums.

We would weight our children, introduce ourselves while waiting and, sometimes, go out straight away from that casual meeting for a cuppa, sharing baby stories, life stories, and laughter. I found this bit in an essay by Brooke Boland:

> *"Shared laughter between women is even better. It has a rebellious spirit and the ability to connect women and draw us closer together. In a culture that, traditionally, works to separate and pit women against one another, shared laughter can be a source of strength."*

But also, apart from sharing baby stuff and laughing and bonding, for support or to fight solitude, women may find themselves bloody angry with the world's injustice towards mothers and children in general. In 2012, when I was pregnant with my second live child, I was approached by a childhood friend who talked to me all about obstetric violence, and asked for help with campaigns about respectful childbirth.

Since then, I have been supporting women's campaigns for better care and outcomes in childbirth, against the formula milk industry, for humanist ways of raising children, with love and support.

Mother activism is a real thing. You may not be creating your own website and lobbying with politicians just yet, but it may as well start with a petition with other mothers to have that baby group open for more than once a week.

Or a round with the neighbours to ask that guy upstairs to stop with the loud parties at this flat after 9pm. As a working mum with a newborn breastfeeding, or if you're continuing education after your baby is born, you might take it up with an employer for flexible working and childcare. It may happen to any of us.

And then, there are the feminist forums at sites like MumsNet. I mentioned them in my previous book, the Grumpy Guide to Radical Feminism. Why do you think they are there? Because feminism is the social and political movement by women, for women's liberation from patriarchy. That's why.

Mother knows best.

Many people think that motherhood online forums are only for their children's needs, but mothers are humans, too. They want to know where they can take their children, what's best for them and how they can raise their children in safety, dignity and happiness.

And for that, they need to know what is available, and what works, from healthy eating, non-violent communication with kids, educational aids, to what their kids future hold.

And that's political.

Get used to mothers taking it up to themselves and challenging harmful practices, campaigning for better ones, for better spaces for them and their children, proper child and mother care, opportunities for children to play and explore, for their safety, children's safeguarding and even mother's rights to some much deserved "me time" - even if that only entails to have someone holding your child for you for a few moments while doing something else. Like going to the toilet alone - a time in which you might even take your mobile phone with you to go to social media. Or an awesome teacher who is holding your child for you, so you can sit a test.

Remember when I said that I was taking a full-time course during my whole pregnancy? I missed so many classes - a bit more than 30% of what I should attend - that I wasn't going to get a certificate for the course. I was studying English for Academic Purposes. I even missed the very last test I should do. I skipped yet another day at the end of the school term, in June, 2008, because the last I knew, the next day was going to be the day of that last exam.

The next day, I went to the college and was told that the test had been on the day before. I was devastated - probably because I was already heavily pregnant and close to my due date. The teacher took pity on me and asked the course headteacher if I could take it anyway, just for myself, and they agreed. The next day, I sat the test. On the last school day, the teacher told the whole class that I scored more than him - and I was granted the certificate. That was a week before my first child was born...

Mother activism can lead to serious activism, too. You may become a Radmum. And the more mother activists, the better, I say.

We are the ones tasked - sometimes solely - to look after these fragile, helpless human beings that we birthed.

We're the ultimate guardians of their lives, whether we like it or not, and that is even when we have a lot of help, which is... quite rare. That's why it can be so powerful when mothers take up activism! We know these little ones of ours, we are with them most of the time, despite all of our little escapades to the toilet.

It can also give us a sense of empowerment in many ways. Being responsible for another life can be quite the step some women find to actually step out of some of the sex roles imposed on women. It's almost like that, when a woman has a baby and faces the music, we feel that we may also want to change the world, one human being at a time.

I could have left this chapter to the end of the book because it talks about the lives of women who became mothers. But I decided that women are too important to be left as an afterthought. We can now carry on to the next chapter, where I'd like to talk about babies again and their first and most powerful survival skill: their crying. It may get on our nerves, but it serves a purpose. And it's inevitable!

Cry baby

Image: Flaticon.com

B abies cry. They have a built-in stereo system to guarantee their own survival. I believe this may be a survival, primeval strategy developed thousands of years ago, to make mothers aware of their needs.

The crying can be strident. And can turn mothers insane. As they grow older, crying truly decreases to a level in which is more "acceptable." It may become less strident, less often and more proactive. But just so.

Babies cry because humans can't talk when they are born. Humans are born quite helpless. Can't walk, can't grab, can't talk. They cry, so mothers can hear them.

But the crying doesn't quite end when kids start grasping how to say words. In fact... crying may be quite a big part of a mother's life for a very long time. Like just poo talks.

Kids who have started speaking may cry, too. It's normal.

The reasons they may cry, though... Yes, they are normal, too. But they can make life quite... interesting.

Young kids may cry because their carer gave them the "wrong cup," - the kid wanted a cup with a specific colour. And then you gave them a cup with that colour that they have asked for, and now they are crying because you have just ruined their lives. Or because you gave them the teaspoon, instead of the tablespoon. Or, as I found out for my own distress, the other way around, when my child outgrew his need for a tablespoon, years later. Silly me to not have noticed.

They may cry because they asked to have ice cream for breakfast and you told them that they should have cereal or bread instead. If you look around "reasons kids may cry," you can find quite the collection.

The child who cried when a parent told them that the Golden Gate Bridge is not actually golden. Or because you put slices of cucumber and tomato on their plate with their macaroni cheese. Or because you "refused" to "switch off the sun" so the kid could light up his Halloween pumpkin.

Or they may cry because you cut off their finger/toe nails, and they would like to have it back, thank you very much.

But you can't. Or may be a bogey that you wiped from their noses, and since it came out of them – at least, that's what I'm assuming, who knows what were they thinking – and now they want it back, too. Or because you flushed the toilet before they could say goodbye to their poo.

Or because they wanted to hold their poo. Oh, see, poo talk is back! Silly me, actually. It never went away.

There are, obviously, good reasons to cry. Like after falling or bumping into something. Actually, I've been told many times that, after a big fall, if a young child cries immediately, especially if it's very loud, there's good reason to believe that this fall might not be serious enough for life long consequences, so checking with the doctor can be a lot less stressful, knowing that you are checking just to make sure!

Be also aware that, for a very long time, mothers – yes, especially them, for we know that most kids spend a longer time with their mothers than with any other carers – will be having to deal with crying, pooping, peeing, bumps, falls, wrong cups/pen/-clothes/food situations until kids overcome them. Keep calm, mother, and pack your survival kits!

My survival kits started as a backpack with nappies, baby wipes, a set of clothes, cloth books/soft toys, water and snacks for me, breast pads, menstrual pads, a guide of activities to do and baby friendly venues to go - like that cinema I mentioned before, or mother/baby yoga classes, mother and baby swimming lessons, mother and babies run-at-the-park-with-baby-in-trolley meetings.

Then... it evolved, like a Pokemon. Soon, I had to pack snacks for the kid, with toys and/or books for entertainment on longer journeys. As the poo chapter shows, it can develop in quite a vision to watch a woman with a young child in a pram. She may have a backpack with all these goods being held at the pram's handles, while also having a small, plastic potty for emergencies, plus a tiny scooter/balance bike, and the grocery shopping in the basket of the pram. Once, I met one of my friends at a park, and our prams were quite impressive, as we also had a container with extra snacks for a picnic, and my friend also had two ginormous, inflated space hoppers when she arrived, a bit late, because the male driver of a bus wouldn't let her on the bus with a child in a pram - yes, society sometimes has a way to really make a mother's life miserable - and she had to walk the rest of the way to meet me.

A baby pram, many mothers will agree, is basically a "child station." When we go out with a young child, we may try to have absolutely everything that they may need while we're out. Including extra sip cups, spoons for yoghourts/pureed fruit and a small first aid kit, with at least a spray to clean wounds and plasters.

I may be of the opinion that many women who can do all that, do so to avoid as little crying as possible!

This may even be a "first world problem," to be honest. Once, I visited some friends in Brazil and we stayed over for dinner. When food was served, I asked my host if she had a "child spoon." At first, she laughed, quite not believing what I was saying. "A child spoon?" she asked? "What is that?" I was a bit taken aback by the question. "You know, a child spoon. A small, plastic spoon that we give to babies and younger children." My friend was also surprised. "I actually never heard of them! Didn't know they existed." So she gave me a tablespoon – at a time in our lives when my child switched and wanted a teaspoon. I was quite apologetic when I quietly and politely asked for a smaller spoon. Even then, my friend was quite not believing it. She never gave a teaspoon to a baby just because they were small human beings.

I guess this was me being told. Things can be and look quite different for other families. I was just trying to avoid my kid inevitably crying, to be honest. This was my second child, who is on the autism spectrum, and it could be quite difficult for me to find positive ways to not be overwhelmed. Interestingly, this mother's youngest child is also on the autism spectrum and she never found herself needing to give her a small spoon.

But then again, we have to acknowledge these kind of things not for being part of the culture. They might not be an actual cultural thing, and yet... all of these baby stuff I had for my kids are affordable in developed countries, but not in places like Brazil. I checked. I checked the prices for really basic baby strollers, sip cups (another unheard item for my friend), teething toys (this one even middle class Brazilian women might not have heard about), baby baskets. In places like Brazil, most mothers have no access to these items at all.

But, back to crying babies. Let's put aside, for a few minutes, the expensive items mothers can afford or can't. There will be sometimes, I believe, that it may not be so good to let a child cry freely, and there may be sometimes that crying is not a big deal.

Sometimes, a breastfeed after a bump may be for comfort, not because the baby is hungry. But breastfeeding a 1 year old child after a bump is not quite the same as giving a dummy to a child after a fall. Breastfeeding could be something for bonding too, while the dummy, many times, will be more like silencing. My opinion, of course, but I'd rather give hugs and a "kiss the owie" than a dummy. Dummies were created to replace the mother's breast when the mother's breast was not available. Do you disagree? That's absolutely fine. It's best that all mothers are able to recount their experiences without judgment and censorship, and this may be something we can all agree on.

Babies may even sleep better if they fall asleep on their mother's breast, which is a habit that does not endanger kids and, quite regularly, they will outgrow in time. But, talking about bedtime routines... this may take longer than a few words. So, see you in the next chapter.

Your new "nightcap" style

Image: Flaticon.com

Bedtime routines. This is your new "nightcap." I know, when we say "nightcap", we are normally talking about that last drink, that nightcap round of drinks, to close the night in big style. But let's be honest: nights out may be out of the table for sometime. At least for weeks after a baby is born. Not that mothers of newborns can't go out. They can. But they might not be able to, actually. They might be too exhausted to go out.

Whatever you do to establish a bedtime routine with your newborn, remember this: you don't actually have to establish a bedtime routine for your child. Sounds crazy? I'll say that again: you don't actually have to establish a bedtime routine for your child. Unless, of course, you need to catch up on sleep yourself. That's how it works.

We create bedtime routines for our children because we, mothers, who may be breastfeeding or bottle-feeding, need to sleep.

So, if you do need to create a bedtime routine, that will depend on your needs and on your child's acceptance of a bedtime routine. It's a two-way factor. Sometimes it's even three, if you have a male partner who is watching something very loud while you are trying to rock your baby to sleep.

You may want to ditch the saying "sleeping like a baby." You may find yourself with a strong desire to sleep like your partner.

Breastfeeding mums may be ahead of this game, in my opinion. Baby's first food (breastmilk) is readily available for the baby, and breastfeeding could - or should - be understood as much more than only food. Sorry for the rhyming. It will happen sometimes. The rhyming, I mean. Anyway, breastfeeding can help with bedtime routine. Babies may fall asleep on the breast, because women's bodies are amazing! At night, breast milk comes with a soothing substance in it, did you know that? Then, in the first weeks, babies may still wake up several times during the night - which is normal - and breastfeeding lying down will soothe the baby and mum can catch up with sleep. But, regardless of breastfeeding or bottlefeeding, a baby can get colic. Sometimes, when they are getting their milk, one way or another, they might build up a lot of gas inside of them. For that, I recommend the burping, if you and your child fancy that. My kids didn't, so I had to resort to something else. What I found it helped was laying down the baby on the bed and make small, slow, circular movements with their legs, as if they were "riding a bicycle." It eases the gasses.

You know, the burping your baby has a purpose. It the gas doesn't come out from the top, it might come out from the bottom. Another tip is holding your baby in what is commonly called the "tiger in the tree" position. That's when you place the baby on one of your arms, with their belly down.

These are all things that can happen to ease a child to go to sleep. Unfortunately, going to sleep is one thing. Sleeping through the night is entirely another matter. It's normal for babies to not sleep through the night for the first months. But here's the thing: has anyone told you that children may not sleep through the night for... years? That you may end up with a child who is 7 and still doesn't sleep through the night? Yup, me neither. But it can and it does happen.

Is there a right time to start a bedtime routine? I don't know. I'd say that, before six months old, if a bedtime routine didn't work yet, it's normal. After six months, babies can be sitting up and crawling, therefore more active, we can say, and then some things can be done. If the baby is still breastfeeding, you can still allow them to fall asleep on the breast, while you put some "white noise" around. My "white noise" was basically my mum working on her sewing machine to deliver her customer's orders.

But now, any smartphone can give you access to an app that delivers a white noise for you to set the scene. Or you may not be sleepy enough and decide to watch a movie. Here, my tip is to turn on the subtitles and turn down the volume to a point that all you and the baby can hear is very similar to a whisper.

Here's the "science" of white noises for babies, if you are interested. When the baby was inside of the uterus, all that he could hear were white noises. Remember that, besides being inside of the uterus, the uterus is filled with amniotic fluid. It's literally like being underwater. You certainly can hear some noises in such an environment, even though you can't actually distinguish many sounds. All you can hear - but you can hear - is muffled sounds. Then, pick up on how the baby might have felt inside the uterus: warm, guarded, safe, in the dark, free floating until they grow big enough to not be able to, but definitely... safe. When you provide that white noise outside the uterus, after they have been born, they will relax.

Simple, right? Especially because it is said that babies have no idea that they have been born during most of their first three months.

The white noise might also come from you singing in a whisper. Anything that can bring back that memory they are born with, of being in this sound-proof, muffled world.

So, dim the lights, crack on with your best 1980s favourite hits - I actually went to the trouble of learning ALL the songs I could that had the word "baby" in it, bare with me, I'm that cheesy - let the baby get that soothing breastmilk at a suitable bedtime and be happy!

For older babies - the ones crawling and sitting, and starting to eat solids - you can try to make sure that they can spend a reasonable half an hour doing some physical activity, maybe before dinner time. Skip a bath/shower to after dinner, give it an hour, then bath. A full but already rested tiny baby stomach, after a bit of physical activity, followed by a soothing bath and a banana for their "nightcap," plus a bedroom in dim lights, a few drops of lavender oil on a pillow and white noise - you might have a fighting chance of making a bedtime routine to work.

An alternative for a soothing essential oil could be a top that you, mum, have been wearing for a few hours.

If the baby falls asleep and you are leaving them on their own cot/bed - or even on your own bed, if you are co-sleeping, while you have a shower and grab something to eat, leave the top next to the baby. Babies know their mother's body smell.

Other alternatives - well, not alternatives, these are more like desperate measures - can include putting the baby in a pram at bedtime, especially during warm nights, and going for a ride outside so that the "bumpy ride" can help soothe the baby. Or a car ride. With the baby, let me clarify. Going for a car ride without the baby will honestly only soothe the mother, so that's not a lot efficient if your aim was to soothe the baby. Unless, of course, you have a male partner that takes over and does the walk with the baby in the pram or takes the baby for that car ride so the mother can put her feet up for some well deserved minutes. Here comes the science: that also can bring back to the memories about the time they were inside the uterus. When the baby was inside, mum was out and about, and the baby was in a kind of very gentle "bumpy ride." Get it?

The real tip here is this: the pram or the car ride work better if, after you notice that the baby has closed their eyes, you keep the ride going for at least ten minutes. That's to establish sleep.

If your baby closes their eyes and you stop the pram or the car a minute later, you may expect the baby to be wide awake in the next minute. So, remember: after the baby closes eyes, keep pushing the pram/riding the car/rocking the baby in your arms/singing "Baby sneezes, mommy pleases, daddy breezes..." for ten minutes.

And then... even then... It might all fail. There will be nights when it all fails.

And if you have an older child besides having a newborn, like I had, you may end up going to your bed with your baby at 9pm, with the older kid in their own bed. Husband is nowhere to be seen - he may as well be sleeping on the sofa in the living room, who the hell cares. You're exhausted. At 3am, the older child wakes up, goes to the living room, lays down on the sofa, forcing his father to go to the kid's bed. Newborn baby wakes up at 5am, feeds, goes back to sleep until 7am. At this point, the husband is up in the living room. I leave the baby with my husband in the living room, take the older child to his bedroom and sleep with him in his bed until 8am.

Or you may end up managing to make a bedtime routine work.

One in which your child is going to bed at a reasonable time, sleeping through the night, even though now you may have an uncanny ability to hear a sneeze or a cough or even your child snoring or laughing during a dream, all of that through closed doors, in the middle of the night, three bedrooms away, while a male partner snores next to you or a washing machine is still working.

Congratulations. Maybe hours of co-sleeping with your child gives you a little bit of rest, even though said child has slept most of the night with their tummies on your face.

Or... they go to sleep at a proper time, sleep through the night but now are wide awake at precisely 6am, like a clock.

And you wake up and get up, hoping that, by waking up at that ungodly hour, and if your child get just the right amount of physical activity to tire out - not to be even fussier - and they have a warm bath, a banana or a glass of warm milk before bedtime, with white noise, dimmed lights, lavender oil, a rain dance, incense, that voodoo a neighbour said it would do the trick, then...

You may hope to establish a bedtime routine.

Just... don't get too discouraged if you don't.

Believe me, this, too, shall pass.

And you are entirely entitled to love all your children equally, but ending up loving, even more, that one who sleeps.

Your new flying options

Image: Flaticon.com

I know, the chapter titles are highly misleading. But in this part of the book, let's talk about baby weaning, baby food, kids food, and picky eaters. "Here comes the plane, zooooom..."

Did you ever use this "technique", by the way? The... plane thingamabob? "Here comes the plane... zooom...open up...opennnn uuuuup.... open up for the plane...now it's flying higher...here it comes!"

Well, did it work?

I decided to start weaning my kids with "finger food:" everything they could grab with their own hands. I started with fruits like sliced bananas and "the Berries" troupe (strawberries, blackberries, raspberries), and then moved on to cucumber sticks. A lot less messy, to be honest, quite healthy and dispenses distracting your kids with screen time combined with the "plane game" to make them open up their little mouths for baby pureed food, that you have to cook and then make it into puree by blending it.

Of course I had doubts about its efficacy. Especially because my second child completely refused to sit in a baby chair – and we had a fabulous one!

At some point, I had to resort to putting his plate on the floor, on the foam mat which he liked to sit on, close to his toys. I felt very ashamed every time I had to do that. It felt like I was feeding the cat. But that's the thing about raising a child: we gotta do what we gotta do. Sitting on the mat, he was safe. Better than forcing him on the baby chair, which he hated and cried a lot while in it, forcing his way out, and risking him falling off the damn, colourful, expensive chair. We ditched the chair.

The real issue is when not even the plane game works. With my first child, at some point, I had to, literally, up my game. It really only works until a certain age, probably around 2 or 3 years, depending on the child. In my case, when the "Here comes the plane, zooom..." wasn't doing it anymore, there was a lot of drama. Not me or him crying, but drama as in "acting up." Doing the job of an awarded Hollywood actress. It would be a bit like this:

"Here comes the plane, zoooooom... here it comes, look at it, there's a plane coming! But, oh no!!! The airport is closed! We can't keep this up, folks, we're running out of fuel! This is a disaster! Mayday, Mayday, plane to control tower, plane to control tower!"

(To which point, I would be standing up, making the "plane"- the spoon with the next bit of food - splutter to show him that the "engine" was failing for lack of fuel. Well, that was the intention anyway.)

"Mayday, Mayday! Plane to control tower, we need to land this plane right now!"

(Here, I could be making the voices of the pilot and the co-pilot talking to each other.)

"Jeff, we need to find another runaway, fast!

Yes, captain. Attention, Tower, flight 101 from Food Airways needs to land now, there's no other way, we're running out of fuel!

Affirmative, plane Food Airways, Mummy Airport is open now for landing, follow instructions."

(That's when I would open my mount and start directing the spoon to MY mouth. At this point, I had made him laugh and, when he saw the spoon nearly engulfed by me, he would - on lucky days - open his mouth.)

There will be accidents.

Food inside the sleeves of the tops. Crumbs and bits of food on the floor, on the chair, on the table. Small pieces of food have a strange habit of getting inside their trousers, tops, even their nappies or on their carers – so many of the times, the mother. But we do what we gotta do.

You might not even have time to eat. You can take your chances, but nothing is guaranteed at this point. You may have to resort to eating – the horror – what they are eating, to save time and to put some food inside of you. Sometimes you may find out that you main diet is to eat whenever your child hasn't finished eating.

On lucky days, you can take the chance that your child suddenly went for an unexpected catnap and, even though you're not even that hungry, you're having your lunch at 10 am because you can have it without hurrying, alone, by yourself, sitting at a table instead of standing up while feeding your child, maybe even watching something fun while eating, and that's seems like a guilty pleasure. For me, it felt like pure adrenalin. Bungee jumping? Parachute jump? That's for the weak. I felt like an adventurer.

Fortunately, things do get better over time.

Fussy eaters - I don't really like the label, but bear with me - may overcome their so-called fussiness in time.

Like everything in motherhood, things do get better. Kids learn to eat different foods, to eat by themselves. To go to the toilet. To help out with the mess, and you may find yourself watching the best magic show you have ever saw, when you went to a room and you saw the floor covered with biscuit crumbs or popcorn, and you asked, like you always do, why the floor was covered with food bits. You did that a million times, you asked them to clean up the mess them made, and they never did. But one day... one day, out of nowhere, your child goes "Oh, sorry, mum! Let me clean that up." And they actually go and do it!

Every stage, it comes and passes. One day, you will be spoon-feeding your child for the very last time. There will be one day that your child will breastfeed for the last time, or they will need you to come and wipe their butts for them for the last time. The last time you washed their hair, the last time they cried after bumping into something without getting seriously hurt, the last time you asked them if they want a "kiss the owie" and they accepted it.

But don't feel despair for that.

With the end of these events, always comes the new phases. The first time they climb steps on a staircase. The first time they eat by themselves. Or try on "grownup" meals.

The first time they laugh after a wee fall and you can laugh together. The first time you go to a restaurant and your child behaves like a wee gentleman, and everybody in the family has a good time, at least. And it becomes a good memory.

The fall-outs can become good memories too, of course. Once they pass, I'm afraid. There's no issue in remembering these little accidents and struggles, in a fond way. You will do that anyway for childbirth, especially if the experience was mostly more pleasant than a nightmare. And then... even the nightmarish experience will fade away over time, because that's what happens, anyway, especially if you managed to have closure about it.

It may be a good thing to treasure these moments, the good and the bad, the processes, the phases, the ins and outs, the ends, the beginnings, after all. They will be part of your shared story together and may help you both to feel connected to each other. Hopefully.

Talking about connection...

Humans also connect to each other with words, apart from known, recognizable gestures. Spoken communication development is such a huge step for humans.

In the next chapter, let's talk about some of the things we can expect when our kids start saying their first words.

Well, I say "let's talk," but we might as well say that it's more like "out of the mouth of babies." Quite literally.

Look who's talking

Image: Flaticon.com

A child's first words are a huge step in their development, no doubt. Many parents expect their child's first words with excitement. Others may expect it with anxiety, hoping that everything goes "according to plan." And when those first words actually come out, it can be a relief.

In many cases, it's best for parents to just go with the flow, I guess. Because language development can take a while. It doesn't start overnight. And it might not start with actual words, but sounds. Babbling is said to be a very important start. Your child is learning how to make out sounds that differ from just plain crying and wailing, which, by all means, it has to be a nice change.

They start repeating sounds that they hear. Even though, it can be said, human babies can already make at least one discernible sound from a very young age. Like, really young, something like from month one after they were born. Apparently, the sound we have for our letter M is a very easy sound to learn. The reasoning for that is because of - drums roll - breastfeeding! I'm not kidding you.

The science of this argument is that many babies breastfeed. It's an ancient sound that humans can make when they are babies.

When a baby breastfeeds, they have their mouth around their mother's nipples. Their lips touch their mother's breast. When they are breastfeeding, they can't make any other sounds apart from mmmmmm. And they do. Try it yourself: put your mouth on the back of one of your hands, lips glued to it. Now, try to say out loud the word "baby" with both of your lips firmly touching the back of your hand. No air can pass. What happened? Were you able to say "baby," or were you saying "mmmm?"

Some people will even say that the word "mother" has the M letter in it, in so many languages, because the sound of the letter M is the sound that babies can make while breastfeeding and, because of that, mothers are associated with breastfeeding. In the sense that it's the mother who will allow a baby to feed and continue to develop outside the uterus. So babies would associate the sound M with breast-feeding and, therefore, the woman breastfeeding them becomes the "Mmmm" person, the woman who feeds them. And later, when babies are hungry, they "know" that they need to breastfeed, so about a month old, they may not cry to ask to be breastfeed or fed with a bottle. Instead, they may start to do the "mmmm" sound! For me, that was a bloody good sign that my kids were ready for breastfeeding.

It worked pretty well, I must say!

But of course, we're all individuals, even when we're still babies, with all kinds of backgrounds and in all kinds of families. M sounds may be first, and they may not. Your child may start babbling with many other sounds, and that's ok, too. What can happen to most babies at some point is that they will be using the sounds they can make to speak about things around them. It may be a while until they can call a duck a duck, to say mom or dad.

Kids may start speaking more intelligible words after they turn one year old and, until they are about two and a half, they may not have spoken words that you know. Some kids, after they start babbling, may learn how to say the sound of things or animal sounds, before they can say the name of that thing itself. They can say "neigh" to call a horse, a "meow" for a cat and a "Tchoo Tchoo" sound for a train. Which is cute and, honestly, bloody useful already.

Their very first "intelligible" word - for an adult, anyway - is another matter entirely. My older child's very first word was "duck." Before mom, dad, cat, dog. Before that, it was all "ba-ba," "da-da," "goo-goo" and similar sounds.

Other kids may have horrified their parents because their first word was "poo" – and variations. A "very hungry caterpillar" might go for "boob".

In some examples I found from other mothers, there were some more elaborate attempts to speak from children. Like the mothers who say that their child's first words were something like "all gone" or "all clean." Mothers and other carers and family members may repeat words or phrases in certain situations and that's what the kids pick up in the end.

Regardless of what will be your child's first word, you're still in for a lot of fun, for all the other words that they will be learning from that moment on.

Because, let's face it, some kids will call things the way they can understand it. Since I'm Brazilian, my two children picked up first the understanding of the Portuguese language – I could speak to them in Portuguese and they would understand it. Nonetheless, the first word my first child ever said was "duck" – not "pato!"

And then, we come to those hilarious attempts to say more complex words.

My second child learned numbers up to ten and the whole alphabet at three years old because of some TV shows with catchy tunes. But this is how he counted: One, "Too," "Tree," "For," Five, Six, "Semen…" At the time of this book, my youngest is 8 years old, and has recently learned what are "Wind Turbines," which he called "Winter Bines."

Although the mixed ups are mostly corrected by some parents, there's no need to worry, or hurry. They will pick it up in due time. Meanwhile, embrace and enjoy the mix-ups. That will too, shall pass. And you're going to miss it!

Shall we go for more funny mix-ups? Kitchen for chicken and vice-versa. Baboons for balloons. Spaguetti seems like quite a hard word for the younger kids, too. Scabetti, anyone? Maybe a Monkey Cheese (Mac and Cheese)? Flavours for favours?

What about those times when kids get it wrong and what they say sounds like a swear word, to the horror of their carers? Some examples I found: cock porn (pop corn); "Can I have some ass in my water?" (the child meant "ice"); "We're going over the bitches (bridges)." "Look at those fuckers (flowers)!" "I'm allergic to penis (peanuts)."

There might also be the case that your kids pick up spoken language skills perfectly. So perfectly, in fact, that this will be when they will be telling other adults what YOU might actually think of them. Kids telling the other adults what they were not supposed to. So you might want to be careful of what you are saying around them, because barely nothing can prevent your child seeing you everyday, as a skinny woman, like in my case, and then when your child sees an overweight person they go "wow, that's a big person." And you want to bury yourself at home and never leave it again.

While researching for this book, I actually found a chart for the first sounds children learn, until they can learn more complex sounds, which you can check on the website Doctor and Dad[3].

The bottom line is: enjoy it while it lasts.

Some mothers not only embrace their kids mispronunciation, but add their "new vocabulary" into the family life. Some might even take it for life and still remember many of them for many years to come. And it can become something nice to remember, or even become an affectionate nickname between family members, as a way of bonding, who knows.

In the meantime, it will crack you up and allow a wave of oxytocin to invade your body with the love you feel for each other.

Until, of course, they do it in front of others and embarrass you - buckle up for that.

You may find yourself spending a long time teaching your child to talk, and then finding out that they are talking non-stop. That's when, when they do stop talking, you become even more alert. Because silence is gold, unless you have kids. Then silence is suspicious.

When all of their cuteness vanishes in the big world, that's when they will show you the real challenges. Like a simple trip to the nearest grocery shop. That's what we are going to be talking about in the next chapter: being out and about with your child.

The end of the world: in the public eye

Image: Flaticon.com

When you have a child, going out takes a whole new level of crazy, I would say. Going out when you are a childless woman can already be hard, if you take my meaning. Think about it: women have to deal with all of those insane expectations imposed on them from the beauty industry. Some women say that they take up to three hours to get ready to go out: hair, nails, clothes, shoes, make-up, accessories, and so on. These expectations come from the women's magazines, the media in general, and even from our workplace policies.

When I was a primary school teacher in Rio de Janeiro, our headteacher threatened me to not renew my permission to work at the school she headed because of the way I dressed. There was nothing wrong with the way I was dressing, I can guarantee you. I was working with kids from a range of 6 to 10 years old, and chose to wear feminine suit trousers, which any secretary would wear to work, combined with a feminine top with a cleavage close to the neck (not loose T-shirts or anything), and flat, fully closed shoes. Instead, I was told to wear a dress, or a skirt and a top with a more "feminine cleavage" (whatever that meant) and shoes with at least some sort of higher heels, combined with a light nail polish, a light shade of lipstick AND small earrings.

All of which harmed me: nails would become breakable, heels would give me a backache, earrings would infect my earlobes. And it was impossible to look after young kids in a dress or skirt - which was the reality: in Brazilian public schools, primary school teachers don't get the luxury of children's inspectors during lunch break. The teachers do that, taking turns so that they can at least have a coffee for ten minutes.

Of course, not all women will be enduring this. But women who manage to be less preoccupied with their appearance and can afford to dress for comfort will still face street harassment and still will have this to worry about, apart from choosing their way carefully from home to work and vice-versa. And all of these, I'm afraid, will still be concerns that women will have after they have children.

But even then, with all of these worries, I still remember what it was like to go out when you are a childless woman. If you don't have to worry about your appearance that much and you live in a relatively safe place, that's how you go out as a childless woman: you get up, get your keys, your phone, make sure you have enough menstrual pads, and leave your flat/house. Right?

That's not what happens after you have a baby.

There's something insidious about the way that nobody tells you that, after you have a baby, you might be afraid of going out with your bundle of joy for the first time ever, all by yourself. Do you know when you have just passed your driving test, and are now in possession of a driver's license? Do you remember what you felt, the sheer terror you were experiencing, the first time you take a car all by yourself and are actually riding it in the real world, instead of the car park where you trained driving with a family member or at a driving school? Well... that's how it may feel to go out with your first child, for the first time, by yourself. You worry that you are going to forget something. That you're not going to make it on time. You worry that something bad is going to happen. But you're going to have to go out someday, right? And you brave it up.

Once the first times of going out are past, and you feel that you have mastered it, here comes the full scale of the situation. You don't even want to get up in the morning anymore. Let alone going out.

You still get up, of course, if you really need to go out.

Then, you go check on your child. Do you need to go out with them first thing in the morning? Then you have to go, wake them up, make them breakfast, hurry them up to eat said breakfast, then pick up clothes and shoes for them, depending on their age and sometimes, on the weather forecast.

If you are like me, you may have a backpack ready with the essentials from the day before. If you are not, then you will have to prepare one. Nappies, baby wipes and a travel changing mat. Water, books, toys. Snacks. Umbrellas, ponchos. Everything you might need outside. A travel potty. Sun cream and summer hat, or woolly hat, gloves, lip balm. Spare clothes for accidents. Bags to contain the infamous "running poos." Plasters. A useful route plan to find the toilets, changing facilities or shops where you can buy stuff you might have forgotten...

Then, you go and get dressed, because you barely slept the night before and your face looks out of place. And you finally start working on getting your child dressed appropriately (warm clothes/clothes for warmer weather). That is, if they let you dress them up. Because your child may refuse to go out, or refuse to let you dress them. A bit like if you were trying to put a sweater on an octopus.

And even when you manage to do all that...

Your child, fully dressed, might refuse to go out, to put their shoes on, they might run away and hide under the bed or in a cupboard, or refuse to leave your home and get in the car, or in the pram, or in the baby sling. And that's going to take you all your repertoire of techniques to convince them to go out, to be able to leave your home with your child. And that's probably not even 7 am.

But, let's just imagine, for the sake of argument, that after all that struggle, you are finally out with your child. Who you put in a pushchair or stroller and is now struggling to get out of it, trying to get up on it, crying because they are stuck on it, throwing their toys out of it, standing up on it. You look around, and everybody is looking at you, as if you were a criminal mastermind torturing an innocent victim, when all you are trying to do is getting from point A to point B with minimum hassle, in the rain, in the snow, or even or on a sunny day.

Sometimes, you just give up, because you are going to be late or you are already late, and you go and take the child off the pram, and now you have a child in your arms, if they still don't walk, plus you are pushing an empty pram with a heavy backpack.

Or you are holding your little one's hand, while pushing the same empty pram – sometimes with a scooter, a balance bike hanging from it or a ball in the pram's basket – and a heavy backpack. Sometimes you do all that while holding an umbrella.

Considering you manage to get out and take your child where you need or want to go, once you are there... Do I need to go on? Children run off their carers. They refuse to hold your hand to cross the street. They refuse to stay close to you. They touch everything they see. They may pick up rocks and dead animals on the way to the place you are going. They may want to put them in their mouth and instantly turn into the fastest land mammals on Earth, because you asked them what they are eating.

Children who are still young toddlers might want to examine thoroughly the many insects, flowers or dog's poo they find on the pavement when you are on a schedule. They might want to jump into puddles, which is another Murphy's Law: the probability of a child finding a puddle to jump in is directly proportional to the days they are not wearing their wellies.

Or they might refuse to get out of the car, or take their time to get out of the car.

But imagine, just imagine, that you managed to get out of your home with your child, braved the streets and arrived at your final destination on that day, without minimum issues. Will your problems end? Of course not. They will still be running away from you and get lost for 15 minutes. They may bump into something and need a plaster. They may cry because they are hungry, or tired, or because they want something that you have no wish to buy right now, and your child may not be old enough yet to understand that they are not having what they want at that precise moment, and may throw themselves on the ground and yell, and cry. They may lay down on the ground and refuse to move. They may go all floppy on you – when they learn that you can pick them up and simply take them where you have to go – and you will have to fully pick them up off the floor, with a heavy backpack, and push an empty pram at the same time. They may take stuff they are not supposed to in shops and throw them on the floor. They may run and fall on their little faces. You may need to put them over your shoulders, while pushing a pram.

And, what if all of it, or most of it, happens in the same outing?

Do you cry, despair? What to do?

My tip is: breathe. You sing it out with a favourite lullaby. You pick up your battles. You throw a little "something, something" to them, so you can get things done. You ignore the crowds who are judging you. They are not in your shoes. You go and do what you have to do. You keep raisins or a favourite toy that can be used to catch their attention and then, when they are distracted, you pick them up off the floor quickly and rush with them, while their little faces look like the face of a cat when it's travelling by car for the first time.

Very rarely, you will get any sort of help when you are out and about with your child. Once, I was with my first child on a bus, and he was crying his eyes off for a reason that is now long gone. Maybe I gave him the wrong toy/cup, who the heck remembers. But he was in his pram, crying, and crying very loud. The bus had stopped at the traffic lights at some point, and it was taking a little while there. I was trying to comfort my child, when I noticed that he was starting to look soothed. That's when I noticed that our bus was "rocking," very gently, slightly up and and down. The bus driver, bless her, was using the bus suspension system on repeat. This system allows the bus to reach the pavement level, so that wheelchair users or parents with prams can get in and off the bus.

By going up and down several times, the entire bus was rocking my child, who stopped crying and fell asleep. Thanks, bus lady!

Another time, close to Christmas, I was doing some late shopping with the same child. When you have to, you go and do so as quickly as you can to avoid meltdowns. I was speedy, efficient, and got everything done in record time. Unfortunately, I couldn't control the public transportation system, and our bus was taking a really long time to resolve. There we were, in the snow, my son and I. Cold, tired, probably hungry too, snacks were not doing it for him anymore, so he was crying, as young kids often do. I was trying to comfort him, lots of cuddles, smiles, offering toys, but he was inconsolable. That's when I started hearing singing. I hadn't noticed, but there was a bunch of people next to the bus stop. They were part of a Christmas choir and had been rehearsing to start soon, I guessed. But then... they actually started earlier. And they were looking at me and my son, singing Christmas songs, and my child slowly stopped crying and started observing them. We all went like that for at least three songs, after which our bus arrived. I approached them, shook hands - yes, they started singing to soothe my child, who was looking curious at them at this point - and we went home with cold feet, but with a warm heart.

The bottom line is: when you go out with a child, prepare for it. You will soon learn what works and what doesn't work with them, the places where you can find help, the places that are child-friendly. It might also help a lot to tell your child exactly where they are going and what it's going to happen on the way there, and why you are going there. I found that this really helped to ease them, once they knew what to expect. This also created mutual trust between us.

And this, too, shall pass. One day, you might have overcome, together, all these little struggles, and a simple trip to the grocery shop doesn't feel like Waterloo anymore. Because kids grow. One day, you might be coming home talking to your children about school or a favourite movie, instead of struggling to catch them up to stay close to you. They do keep us on our toes when they are little. It takes stamina. We might as well talk about fitness, then. For you and for them.

Any way, shape or form

Image: Siipkan Creative from NounProject.com

How does a woman keep in shape and mentally sane after they have children? It's important for women to know that their bodies can change dramatically during pregnancy, and that's ok. Most things can go "back into place," anyway: the baby bump can reduce, you may not keep the weight you put on during pregnancy. Or you may. But if there's one thing that will keep happening, as you could see in the last chapter, is that kids will keep you on your toes. That may feel like going to the gym for 8 hours a day. Only, if you were doing that, that still doesn't feel as tiring as looking after a child for three hours. Many women may say that, after having a child, they never felt so tired, and that they would easily run a marathon, if they didn't have kids.

Walking can be a good source of energy. I find that the more I walk, the better I feel to keep up with young children. Or any other favourite physical activity you like. You know, apart from running after your kids – sometimes it feels like it's a whole new type of sport's category. Which, in a way, can be good for them, too. If you are lucky, they may tire out for the night, you know. If you are unlucky, they will be teary at bedtime because they are too tired. As everything, it can all go wrong in the blink of an eye.

The other thing about health, of course, is mental health. I mean, how do we not go insane when we have so much on our plates? When we are juggling some many balls up in the air? Many women who work from 9 to 5 will have many other issues to deal with after they have children. Deadlines, childcare, breastfeeding in the workplace, the workload in general - the one at the office and all the rest that still need to be done at home, of course, to start with. Basically, at the end of the day, if you made enough money to pay all the bills, kept your kids alive and had a shower, it feels like you climbed Mount Everest. Twice this month.

Many women have said it, and you can ask around to confirm, but sometimes, women focus on work after having children because all the struggle they have ever faced in a job has no comparison with the level of physical (and emotional) strength required to look after a child.

That's when a mother takes longer than usual in the toilet, not because she has a massive number two, but because she needs two minutes of peace - and it feels like a holiday. Even if she doesn't have a job. Or a woman who used to hate flight delays starts to think of them as a luxury, so that she can spend a little more time all by herself.

All of that, of course, on very little sleep. I found a quote recently that said: "working moms are guinea pigs for an experiment to show the world that sleep isn't really necessary for humans."

But I digress. Let's have a look at the basics at home. What do we do when we have a child? In the first days after the arrival of a newborn, we may not feel the need for much, just now, because newborns are notoriously stationary. Which doesn't last long, it has to be said. In a few months, when they start crawling, you might want to babyproof your home. Cupboards, wall sockets, doors wedges, putting everything breakable on higher shelves, covering the floor with foam mats, getting a plastic cutlery set. Plastic plates, plastic cups. Which many of us, adults, will still be using for ourselves too, sometimes for years to come because, let's face it, it's just easier. Your child may not only be dropping their cutlery and their plates and their cups on the floor, but they will be dropping yours, too.

And yet, accidents can still happen. Pieces of furniture with sharper edges, corners, drawers and door frames everywhere are well known magnets of children's heads, arms, legs. It's like Murphy's Law: the sharper the surface, the greater the chances of your child bumping into it.

Some parents may feel like they need to babyproof nature, just to avoid the most of it, and they are not wrong, but all I can say is: children find ways to get hurt.

You might find yourself carrying plasters in your pockets, and a child with five to ten plasters on a leg.

Kiss the owie.

And try to not make a big fuss out of it, either, unless it might be serious, like ANYTHING ON THEIR HEADS. Head bumps require a bit more attention. And I mean, any head bump. Unless your child is not bleeding, not sleepy and looks alert and can be distracted easily with a toy or a lullaby. Anything else that is not bleeding and your child can stop crying in a few minutes, relax, give them a big hug, kiss the owie – and get the plaster.

If you can manage to avoid most of it at least, there will still be things you can't avoid, like colds. They may be worrying, surely. But if you have a healthy child, most illnesses can be dealt with swiftly. Depending on where you are, there are cough syrups and pain relief. That is, if your child accepts medicine.

Mine didn't, most of the time. I found myself resorting to lots of more natural methods. Eucalyptus drops to ease their breathing when they have a blocked nose. Bananas for diarrhoea. Lemon juice for tummy aches or headaches. Honey for sore throats, warm baths to regulate the body's temperature when they have a fever. Another trick I learned was to put a rub ointment (like Vicky Vapor rub) on the soles of their feet, then cover their feet with socks. It helped to avoid the night coughing.

And of course, you worry about their diet, the amount of physical activity they do, their socialising with other children, their skills development. It's all part of the deal. Big spaces like playgrounds might be the solution to keep kids in shape. Short walks in parks and woods, and then longer and longer walks, might keep you both in shape, with energy, good bonding and in good mental health. Quality time, playing together when it's possible, developing your connection, and yes, having unhealthy treats every once in a while, it's all valid, me thinks. You may be able to cook healthy meals most of the time, but you may not have the time. It's all good.

When a woman becomes a mother, that's not the end of the story. It's only the beginning. She becomes a carer of another human being. A nurse. A teacher.

A therapist. An air traffic controller. An event organiser. Driver. A sudden explorer and researcher - and a bloody good one at that. It's a full time job, no doubt. Some women feel that looking after their children and their home becomes their full-time occupation, and that their job is a "side gig." Some say it's a job that doesn't require experience, doesn't give any training, there are no wages to be earned, people's lives are on the line, and yet, you can't quit.

And it's bloody tiring. You might not have time for a coffee. Maybe an iced coffee. You know, when you make coffee, but your kid called you, and you forgot you made a coffee, and then you reheat the coffee somehow, but now you forgot it again because the washing machine finished the washing cycle, or you had to finish work, and you forgot it again, but you really wanted a coffee, and now you're too tired to make another one or to be able to remember that you reheat the coffee, so you drink it cold.

And all of that, of course, it's BEFORE your kids even start going to school. Which is a whole different phase. We shall get on to it, then, in the next chapter.

School of life

Image: Monkik from NounProject.com

Children's education has to be one of the most annoying things about motherhood, in my opinion. When we get to this point in a child's life, women can be assured that they have already had their fair share of guilt, pressure and being blamed for whatever happens to their kids. We deal with that whether we choose to offer a dummy or not, breastfeed or bottle feed, using cloth nappies or disposable ones, staying with kids all day long or going back to work, the kind of food we offer them, the kind of attention we give them. Anything goes to blame mothers, at this point. Mothers every move is now fair game for public scrutiny. So, this couldn't be different when it comes to what we went for in terms of our kids' education.

Many times, a woman doesn't have any other choice but to enrol their kids in the nearest school. Almost very rarely, we can choose their school carefully. That is, when we have the means to do so. That means, money. Which is something as rare in most mothers' lives as hen's teeth. Most mothers - even middle class - struggle with money. You hear mothers telling their children all the time that they are not "made of money." Even though Made Of Money may be shortened as M.O.M. People don't actually believe that the sex pay gap exists, even though it does.

Assuming you are able to choose a school, suited - as far as you can see - to your child needs - you still are in for a lot of headache. Like everything else, after considering schools for weeks, even for months, it's registration, buying their school gear, including uniforms, school bags, sports' kits, their stationery, lunch boxes, and school books. Mothers who can't choose their kids school, by the way, still have to do it all, of course.

Then, you have to time carefully their school days, whether you work or not. If you work, you may need to deliver your child before school starts. Every woman who is a mother knows that, because work still starts at 9, even though school may start at 9, too. I know, right? Insane. I find it a bit daft that more people do not see the amount of reproductive labour that is on women's shoulders and that most workplaces policies were not made thinking of women who are mothers.

Even when you time everything with startling accuracy... you might still forget something. Have you ever sent your child to school without their water bottle, the rain trousers or the wellies the teacher asked you to send? Or, the mother of all horrors, without their lunch box? I did. In fact, during the week I was writing this chapter.

I mean, I didn't actually send my child to school without any food, but he had a picnic that day and, when in standard mode, I sent him his normal meal, instead of "picnic" stuff, like finger food and snacks. I only found out my mistake when I picked him up, at the end of the school day, when I had to wait for him to finish the meal I sent him.

I say, if they go to school with the very essentials, I don't care about anything else. Sometimes, sending their homework (still incomplete) back to school already feels like you achieved something. At least their jotter is not in a toy box this time, almost lost forever.

You have a lot of other things to worry about, anyway. Like how your child will be labelled at school by the other children and the school staff. If they are eating their lunch and not getting stuffed up on candy that the other parents are sending for their kids to school. If your children are getting along with the other kids and the school staff. If they made friends. Even if they are missing you.

And that all may come way before you even think about whether they are learning anything at all at school.

And that's how, after becoming a mother, a nurse, a teacher of early years, a driver, an event organiser, a researcher, a therapist and so much more, mothers may also become special agents. Bloody 007.

I spy with my little eye, all the other mothers at the school gate, while waiting for my kid to come out. You start your research. You eye the other mums - yes, you heard that right, most parents at the school gates are also women, whether they are mums or other carers.

You may hide behind a bush, a tree or a car. You are observing the other women in their element – ok, fair, in their element in patriarchy, with women's reproductive labour solely on women's shoulders. Nothing is more telling than the school gates. Women arrive, one by one. They may be looking at their phones, or they have a book with them. They may just be standing there, looking bored, at least in the first school days of the school term. Coming the next few days, it will be a whole different story. It may even start on your child's very first day at school.

You start spotting the mums. You may label them, according to the best patriarchal manuals. The working mums, the stay-with-their-kids mums.

The "helicopter" mums, the "soccer mums." The mums who come to the school gate in sport's gear, or the mums who come on a bike with a child bike seat or a bike trailer. If you're lucky enough, you may even spot a Goth mum - rare, but not yet extinct - or a hippie mum. If you are unlucky, you may be me, also during the same week in which I forgot to pack "picnic" snacks, who arrived at school and felt something touching my arm. I thought it was a mosquito. I looked down and saw, to my horror, a clothes tag. Reader, I was wearing my short sleeved top on the inside out.

You also observe their kids, too. The ones who come to the gates with their classmates, because you have your eyes on the prize: nice kids that you can invite for a playdate at home after school or during the weekend to take your child away from screens, or to invite them to your child's upcoming birthday party. You basically became, at this point, your child's Head of Human Resources.

And then, only then, you might start thinking - and worrying - about your kids educational needs. That's when they start coming home with homework to do and they refuse to do it, or find it too difficult and cry, and you are sending your child back to school the next day with their homework incomplete.

Which will instantly reflect on how bad of a mum you are, apparently. Or when you go to a parent's evening and you never see school work hanging on their classroom walls with your child's name on it. Or when you find out that your child still can't read or write, even though it's already the middle of the school term, and you made a monumental effort with the homework, and the teacher tells you that your child is behind his classmates. Can you still see the light at the end of the tunnel at this point? Is there any hope?

Once, my first child wrote something on a paper, which could only be described as a scribble. When I asked him what he wrote, he said that he wrote: "We have to go to my friend's house, otherwise we will be destroyed." I never laughed so hard in my life. Honestly, I wasn't that worried anymore. With this level of imagination, I was sure that he was going to be alright.

When you get past those initial fears about the school environment, your child's safety, their learning and well-being, there will be other things that can be happening. School is not only the place where your child goes daily. It's a place where a mother might be going quite frequently, too.

There will be all the chatting at the school gates with the other parents, especially among mothers. Contrary to what most people believe, these conversations will vary greatly, from school policies, a planned trip or kids' camps for the school holidays, to work. Or... it could completely unrelated to a woman's kids. Yes, that's right, women don't always just talk about children when they get together.

I remember one day, when me and two other mothers were talking - rightly so, about our work/jobs, when that rarest of creatures arrived and joined us: a father who was picking up his child. They appear out of nowhere, sometimes, always coming to the school gate as if they are doing this very important job, including boasting about how great of a father they are. This one approached us that day and instantly started making conversation. After we greeted him, he went on and on about children's rearing stuff. I believe that he genuinely thought that we, as women who were mothers, would be only talking about motherhood, and that by giving his two pennies about how HE was raising his child, that he was "bonding" with women by speaking what he thought we were talking about. When he actually had just interrupted three women who were talking about careers and other personal things.

Bloody entitlement and bloody sexism, to think that the only thing a mother talks about is child rearing.

And then, we may come to all those occasions when parents are required to actually be inside of the school, apart from parent's evenings. I'm talking about the school shows for Christmas, the Sports' Days, Mother and Father Days, or whatever events the school comes up with to "involve" parents in our kids school life and show to parents how clever their kids are. Other parents do that all the time too, to be honest, especially in the infamous, dreadful, feared, Parents WhatsApp groups. That's when you may find out a whole other side to the types of mums that exist. There will always be the woman who can't stand a silence gap in the group, constantly greeting the other members in the morning, sending inspirational quotes, bringing ideas for play, cooking and similar.

There will be the mothers who are mostly silent, or the ones who are constantly concerned about everything in the world, from wars, to junk food and the postal service. The mums who have the entire school year planned, while you barely remembered to sign the permission for the school trip that is happening the next day.

The activists mums, who will suggest taking up to the regional education board the concerns anyone might have. The social media mums, and the mums who boast about their kids' achievements. Like the day they had a sleepover/camping at school (my kids used to go to a small montessori school) and, the next day, the mums were boasting on how their kids had so much fun that the next day, they crashed as soon as they got home, not even reaching their bedroom, while you are gritting your teeth because it's 10pm now and your child is still wide awake and hyperactive after all the fun.

Whatever happens from now, mothers will be exposed to the school and the other parents' scrutiny as "good/bad parents." The always late mums. The mums running the show, organising the stall at the start of the school year to exchange school uniforms. The mums who don't interact that much. The stylish mums. There will be judgment, so try and keep your head up. Focus on what is best for your child. You already have a lot on your plate - never forget that. You are doing your utmost best.

Choose your battles - and your priorities. Make lists if you need to. Find out what your child actually needs to learn, and try to make school work for both you and your child.

Also... as a qualified primary school teacher myself, let me tell you something: if a child is not learning that much, it's never the child's fault.

Many other things can be deciding factors for that. A child might need glasses. Their teacher may not be that well qualified, of course. The school might lack resources. But, most importantly, if you feel that most conditions for learning are met and your child is still not learning... I say that honestly, and as a primary school teacher myself: it's the educational system's fault. Not to point fingers at all, but that's the reality. That's why it is so important to find a school environment that suits both mother and her children.

I even did homeschooling with my kids for a while, to be honest. I focused on their writing, math skills, general science and general world history.

They will get there, in the end.

I did that because I thought they needed to spend their youngest childhood years with a bit more spare time for creativity, fresh air and less pressure to do exams.

A personal choice, of course.

When considering sending them back to school, I was able to make some financial sacrifices to enrol them in Montessori schools, because more than having high achievers who score high in school exams, I wanted them to be able to read books - and wanting to read books. To be curious, to expand their vocabulary, to be able to write intelligible messages, to know the world around them, to be able to use maths in day to day life, to feel safe, happy and welcomed in a school environment and, of course, to make friends and have meaningful interactions with other children.

You want your kids to thrive, not only to survive and grow older. Speaking of which... We might be approaching the end of this book. But of course, motherhood doesn't end when your kids grow older. It may become easier over time, if you are lucky. If you are not lucky, you may still have your children with you until their 30s. Sorry to scare you. Anyway, let's talk about kids growing up, for the bad and for the good of it.

Growing season

Image: Valeriy from NounProject.com

K ids grow, right? There's nothing stopping it. Kids have this really unpleasant habit of not fitting anymore in their clothes when you least expect it.

For that matter, when you are a woman planning to have a baby, there will be a lot of clothes/shoes relating things to consider. To start with, the baby's layette. Funny thing about it is that I had my two children in an English speaking country and I never heard of the name "layette" before. I think I just called them "baby's stuff."

Anyway, the main point is that kids can grow quite fast. There's no point in stuffing yourself with expensive baby clothes and with a lot of them of the same size when you have a newborn. As a matter of fact, that can be said for any other age, to be fair. First, because they will outgrow it really fast. Second, remember the accidents. It's not even only the running poo. Babies drool, babies throw up breast milk, formula milk. When you start weaning them off, at about six months, they will make all kinds of mess with their food.

When they grow slightly older and are crawling, or already walking, then there will be mud. Muddy puddles. More food. Painting. Sand.

Before potty training, here comes the poo and the pee again, sticking to their clothes and staining it. The blood from the bumps and the falls and, of course, all the clothes tearing on the knees from the falls, or from kids biting their tops' sleeves, or the hens and the hoods and the sleeves that get caught on furniture and tear away.

But you will get the hang of it, eventually.

You will learn that what you really need is to have enough clothes and shoes for all the situations that may come your way. Which can be a bit tricky when your child goes through their growth spurts.

There may be a sudden change in weather conditions, like a sunnier and warmer day when it's still winter, with double-digits temperature, and your child might as well benefit from a bit of sunshine.

Only, their summer clothes don't fit them anymore.

Or it could be the other way around, and suddenly you have to rush to the nearest department store to buy your child new snow boots so they don't freeze while going to school, or they need wellies for when it's raining, and so on.

You may also suffer from an utter lack of storage space at home and, like me, has to resort to arrange your children's clothes in the spring, putting away the winter clothes in a box, like trousers, heavy coats, gloves, woollen hats, snow socks, and leaving available to them only the short sleeved tops, shirts, bermuda shorts and socks suitable for warmer temperatures.

Which, of course, you are going to have to do all over again when it starts to get chilly outside because, as we all know, coats and sweaters are pieces of clothe you wear when your mother feels cold.

And of course, you may think you finally have everything under control: your kids have enough clothes - you think - and the right clothes for the time of the year. They might even have new clothes to go out - fancy that! You have just bought them new clothes for the season, you were all proud that your kids are finally going to be able to be sporting non-stained, pristine looking clothes when outside the home, when the weather suddenly changes again and you have to take some of the winter/spring clothes outside of the box/piece of luggage you put them in earlier. And then, two weeks later, the day is finally here. A sunny day, with brand new clothes.

Only... your child had another growth spurt during that time, that you haven't actually noticed, and their brand new shorts don't even pass their hips, or their tops don't even pass through their heads. And your despair.

The solution to that, of course, is to buy clothes ever so slightly bigger than they actually need. You might also want to think of hitting the cheapest shops for clothes to be used for "heavy playing," and having some good spares for birthday parties. There are also many kids clothes available that allow for kids constantly growing, with adjustable waistlines on trousers and shorts, but I could never get this bit quite "right," to be honest. I mean, I try my best to have all the necessary garments for every season, but most of the time my kids are still either wearing clothes that are still too big for them or too small. The very few times my kids are wearing clothes that fit them perfectly last not much longer than two weeks, when they then, suddenly, have another growth spurt out of nowhere and outgrow everything they have – again.

And of all these, of course, it's only clothes. After all, growth spurts come with a whole new range of pain. Sometimes, literally pain. Growing pains.

Some even might notice a rise in temperature in their children. Mood changes. Probably in both of you. There are some signs that may help parents - as we all know, most of the time - mums - to detect when a growth spurt is coming. An increased appetite is one of them. That's when you have already fed your child four increasingly big meals on a certain day and they are still at the fridge's door, looking for something else to eat, especially before bedtime.

They may also be sleeping slightly longer, and if you are anything like me, you may feel the need to check if they are still breathing, because you can't just believe that they went to bed at a totally reasonable time at night and, nonetheless, they are still asleep at 7am in the morning.

Apart from all that, there's all the emotional, sometimes heartbreaking, changes in their appearance. Losing their baby cheeks and dimples, their arm/leg chubbiness.

Then, losing their child-like looks.

Becoming taller than you in their 11-13s and having to buy adult clothes/shoes for them, which don't come anymore with adjustable waistlines and, quite frankly, don't even fit your child properly.

But you end up with having no other choice but to get abnormally bigger clothes for your kid rather than forcing them down in the tight kids' clothes in which they don't actually fit anymore. And not being able to find shoes with Velcro in the adult section for a child who is nearly your height but can't do shoe laces just yet.

Starting puberty.

Fortunately, I would say that there is also other stuff to look forward to. They may lose their initial kind of cuteness, but surely other things come into place. Especially when it comes to the things they start to be able to do for the first time. That's part of growing too, of course. Their little achievements. The first time they climb stairs, ride a bicycle, speak, and go to the toilet completely by themselves. The loss of their first initial cute looks always comes with a new acquired skill, believe me. Because they are growing.

Curiously, while our kids are growing right in front of our eyes, developing new skills, exploring the world, discovering themselves and whatnot, we may find that mothers may regress to childhood a little bit. No, I'm just kidding. Women do not regress to childhood when we have a baby.

But we might surely adapt to a child's needs in many ways, including in the way we talk and behave every day.

In the next chapter, I'd like to explore a bit of the so-called "mom talk." You know, when women who are mothers take over the world, a mom talk shall become sacred again. Listen to mums, folks.

Mother knows best!

Mom talk

Image: P Thanga Vignesh from NounProject.com

At this point, you might be thinking that we are going to talk about all those very common and familiar phrases that many women adopt when they have children. You know, the "Don't Make Me Come in There!", the "If all your friends jumped off a bridge, would you?", or the very mean one, the "Stop crying or I'll give you something to cry about."

Those are all examples of mom talk, of course, and you may as well have used them. Or will. Or won't ever use it. But there are certainly other variations out there, no doubt. Mom talk - and mom behaviour - might as well not only be these common phrases for when your kids misbehave. Sometimes, when women become mothers, they may find themselves thinking so much about their children, other people's children, and everything else related to child rearing, that it takes over all other aspects of their lives.

After all, you are going to spend a substantial part of your day time - and, the goddess help us, even night time - with your child or children. Spending time with them will require you talking to them, playing with them, cooking for them, cleaning up after them, singing to them, taking them to baby and kids' activities outside home, reading for them or with them, watching stuff with them.

To their despair, mothers may find out that many or most of the time spent with their children start to affect all other areas. Women have started retaining many words, phrases and behaviours they resorted to while they were spending time with their kids. You may find yourself adopting a very special way of talking. You may start referring to stomachs as "tummies" or "bellies," bruises as the "owies," adults as the "grown-ups," nasal mucus as the "boogers." There are many other examples of "baby talk," or "children-led speech," also called by some people as "motherese" or, for brainiacs, the "infant directed speech," that you may find yourself doing to boost your child's speech and to bond with them through communication.

Many experts in child development may say that "baby talk" is actually good for your kid. The issue is, surely, when a woman starts taking that to the other areas of her life. Like when a mother sees someone tripping on a rock and says "Upsy Daisy!" Recently, a woman said on a popular social media that she was doing a breast ultrasound. She recounted that the technician, a woman and a mother herself, put the gel on the wand and said to her: "Here comes some warm jelly!" And, after that she proceeded to do a "whoosh-whooshing" towards her breasts like an aeroplane.

To which, the woman explained, the technician stopped, "mid-whoosh," and finally said that she was sorry for that, but she had twin toddlers and was exhausted...

We all do it, at some level. Or might not do it at all. Mothers do what they have - or can - do.

The goddess knows I have done it. With my kids, I call meals "yummy yummy time," and I have no shame to say that I have actually said to other adults, coming for dinner, when it was "yummy yummy time!" Or the time you turn to your family doctor and say that you have a tummy ache.

In other cases, women may be seen avoiding swear words when talking to their children, and instead adopting variations that are, frankly, hilarious. "Poo on a stick," "Son of a biscuit," "For fox sake" and "Shut the front door" might be among my favourites. At the school gates, at the softplays and the museums, you can see it playing out in the wild. A sea of "potty mouth" mothers cursing their way out with their "what the frogs," their "fudges," their "clustterfluffies" and their "holy molies."

There are also the common behaviours you can observe to spot a woman who has children.

They may be like me and carry a backpack, instead of purses and bags.

Remember the "child station" I spoke about earlier? My backpack is now a place where you can find children's snacks, baby wipes for "snot" emergencies, and plasters. There are always toys in my bags. You promise to bring something to someone, like a book, and they have to wait a few minutes until I find it in the middle of all of that kid's stuff. And when I finally find what I'm looking for and pull it out, there will be toys and wipes and building blocks that I picked up in the morning and forgot inside the bag flying around like confetti.

Or you have a friend visiting and you tell them to help themselves to a cold drink from the fridge, and they find a soft toy next to it.

You open the drawer on your desk at home, or in the cupboard in the kitchen, or in your bedside table, and there will be cars, pieces of games like dominoes or jenga, rocks, dried flowers your kids gave you, lost cards from the deck of cards that you used to enjoy playing but your children have no interest in indulging you. Strings, crayons, elastic bands in your pockets. Dinosaurs in the bathtub. Marbles inside of your shoes.

Building blocks - the very tiny ones - everywhere, but especially in unsuspected places on the floor, ready for you to step on them. In the creases of the sofa, or under the pillows on your bed. Your life turns into a sea of toys, bibs, burp cloths, and baby wipes popping up everywhere.

This is all part of women's reproductive labour. It's not only gestating, giving birth and breastfeeding. It's all the emotional work that takes place after said child is born. Like knowing where your children's clothes, shoes, favourite toys and safety blanket are, every single time. Well, I say this, but we might as well say that this is about knowing where we have placed them in the first place, because in a home with children, everything that can be out of place can be put back into place twice a week, but then they are always capable of being, mysteriously, everywhere again in the next hour. And of course, nothing, ever, is completely lost forever, unless a mother can't find it. Then, yes, then it's lost.

In the first place, you resorted to putting your children's stuff in certain places so they could find it again easily, instead of having to endure your child's endless quests of "Mum, did you see my dinosaur?" - which was driving you nuts.

You did the same thing with their clothes and shoes because, otherwise, you tell them to get ready to go out, and they are picking up ALL the stained, ragged garments that you have kept to be worn for when they want to go to the playground. Because there's no way you are going to let them go to the playground and go straight to the sand pit with the brand-new tops and shorts and trousers that you have reserved for parties.

Because the last time they were invited to a party, they were wearing a top with a tear under the armpit, or a pair of trousers with a hole on the knees, or socks with their toes out.

What can also happen is that you start doing that at work or in a shop you went to. You start arranging them too, don't you? If that's the case, ask yourself if you are doing it for habit, or because you feel like doing something, anything at all, that does not relate to being a mom, just to feel alive.

You do it because you have too, especially if you are the main provider in your family.

You do it even if the father of your child lives in the same home.

Because there's no way a woman can have a career, or have minimum me-time, when a mother is left alone to do all these things without any other help.

Plus, changing nappies, making meals, tidying up, breastfeeding or making the bottle for bottle feed, researching the colour of your child's poo and pee, booking doctor's appointments, planning a play-date, sending a pestle and mortar to school for an art's class, picking up your child, telling them bedtime stories, asking about their day, playing with toy trains or cooking sets, while also picking up towels left on chairs, beds and sofas, setting the table, putting clothes to wash, hanging them to dry, collecting them after they have dried and folding them to go into the wardrobes.

You do it so you can breathe, every once in a while, because everything can or could be in place, easily reachable, and neither you or your child go crazy on each other.

You may as well function quite well in the middle of this chaos, because you are kind of a layback person.

Congratulations, then.

I can't even remember my keys when I leave. I have

to tingle them about ten times to make sure they are in my hand before I finally close the door of the flat, because the door of the flat locks when closed, and can only be opened again with the keys. And if you forget the keys inside the flat and close the door, especially when you work from home and the only time you are leaving home is to pick up your kids at school, you are not only going to be locked out of your flat. You are going to be locked out of your home with two hungry children, moaning in the stairways, waiting for the landlord to arrive with spare keys, sometimes with no food, no water, in a winter cold corridor for an hour. Which, as most mothers must know, it can feel like a week or so.

Mom talk, here, it's not only the common phrases you might hear mothers saying. It's motherese: it's all the little and the big things, sacrifices and deeds that a woman do to survive after having children and to guarantee that their children thrive. Would you agree?

The bottom line

We can say many things about motherhood. That motherhood is hard, or it's chaos, or that motherhood is emotionally draining. It's also compulsory in patriarchy, did you know?

I chose to talk about being a mother when you really want to be one, for comedy purposes, but we do have to consider two other aspects.

On one hand, not every woman can or want to gestate a baby or adopt a child. That's ok, right? Many women do want to, and many women won't have a choice in the matter, let's be honest. On the other hand... all human beings who have ever been born, came out of a woman. You, me, everyone. Motherhood will keep happening, unless, of course, humans already came to some sort of unspoken agreement where it was decided that it's time for humans to be wiped out from the face of the Earth and, as often happens to mothers, no one told us.

So, this book is for all women who have gestated all the human beings who have ever been born, and also to all the women who adopted children and raised them. Because, from the moment a baby or a child is in this world, we have so much in common. We have chaos, yes. We have the struggle, yes. We might even have fun. Fun? Maybe. Why not? What would be the most fun you can have after having a baby (or adopting a child)?

Bets are all out, but choosing a child's name can be something. Unless, of course, you are from a country that has pre-approved names, like Portugal. Fair, being from Brazil, there can be some reasoning to that. After all, parents may choose absolutely insane names for their kids. Honestly, some parents name their children, I don't know, Table, Chair, Spoon. Crazy stuff like that. In Brazil, it is very common to have names that are a combination of the father and the mother's firt name. So you may end up being the child of Mary and John, and they name you Joma or Majo. Or variations of well accepted names, like me. Very few people would spell my name as Andreia - the most common spelling is Andrea, even in other languages. Which was my dad's doing, by the way. Basically, I'm lucky that my mum convinced him to not name me Andreya.

Do you ever manage to have fun with your child/children as well? It may not be very often, but it can happen. Women who are mothers are not a monolithic bunch. There will be women who love playing with their kids, and the mothers who find playing with kids quite boring might frown upon them. And many women, of course, might have fun at their child's expenses - secretly, of course. We don't want to mess our kids up much more than the absolutely inevitable. This one may even happen a little bit more often than we think, if I'm honest. I mean, have you seen them, those little ones you have at home? Kids may say and do the craziest things, often demanding the impossible, and driving you insane in the process. Of course we feel like having a go at them every now and then. Otherwise, most of us would be branching out sooner and running away.

Making fun of your kids is more common than we think, and it may happen in the most innocent of ways. No, I'm not advocating for mothers to make fun of their kids. I'm just saying that sometimes it happens, yes. Like, when you give all of what you've got for a child, for so long, that you forget your own needs and, all of sudden, they reach a new phase in their development and stop needing you for something that has been a constant for months.

And now, they are doing something by themselves, and you end up "missing" the time when you had to be doing stuff for them, and you haven't just yet figured out what to do with the few extra minutes you gained. That's when you see your child watching a new episode of a favourite kid's show without blinking, and you get bored and start throwing soft toys close to him to see if he wants to play, instead of watching.

You might have fun with them when you see their achievements. Sorry, I meant pride. It might be fun but, in reality, it's mostly pride. Or relief, because now that they can do some things, you don't have to do it for them. But also pride. You are proud of what they can do, of what they can achieve. In reality, you should also be proud of yourself. Give yourself a pat on the shoulder. You did it, you really did it. You may feel proud that your child taught you how to use social media or a new electronic device, if you are in your forties or fifties now, but you can be proud that you taught them to use a spoon.

You can be proud that you have become a mother and raised a whole new human being. That's a part of you, even though you, as a woman, have so many other awesome aspects about you.

You may have a career, you may have accomplished many things, and you raised a child.

Or... you may have raised a child and didn't have a career, and you should be proud that you raised another human being, who you looked after, cared for and had, or have, fun with. Who cares what other people think? They are not in your shoes. You do what you have to do when you have a child to raise. Your choices are your own, even though most times it looks like you didn't have many choices.

You have faced judgement, backlash, hardship, and now you are here, a mother. Mothers can be the most organised bunch of people who have ever walked on Earth.

Mothers used to be in small communities in pre-history with other women, knowing that a baby was coming, and creating pottery to collect food for when the baby arrived, so we wouldn't have to go gathering food with an offspring that we would need to take everywhere with us, as human babies are born quite helpless.

While their biological fathers were scattered in the forests, eating insects and barely speaking.

Women created language, named stuff, conquered fire, created needles to make clothes and protect themselves and their kids from the cold, built huts to escape wild animals and to be in a warm place with a newborn, created agriculture, invented cooking and all the fundamentals of science as we know it.

And all of that, we created so that we could guarantee the survival of our species, through the survival of our offspring. We did all that, in order to ensure that our kids could survive and grow into adulthood, so our species would succeed.

Every human was gestated inside of a woman's uterus, and and every human being was born out of a woman. Mothers conquered nature first, to ensure that nature would not take their children away. Mothers think of the future, because we know that the future is coming with our children. Human mothers evolved to care for their young and ensure they would survive - unfortunately, with a few "blips" in the way. I mean, what's with all this "human evolution", when mothers still only have two hands?

And even then, if mothers could rule the world again - oh, yes, the world was ours before, a long time ago - we could live in more peaceful times.

Isn't that what we do in all the playgrounds, soft plays and kids birthday parties?

Ensuring that everyone is having a good time and is playing nicely?

Give mothers their due credit. Mothers know best.

Mothers know what is good for their children, mothers know their children.

> *"My sister said once: 'Anything I don't want Mother to know, I don't even think of, if she's in the room."*
> *- Agatha Christie*

And, of course...

Don't make us go in there!!!

People will keep trying, of course. Starting fights and wars, I mean.

But mothers must stay firm.

People might ask their mothers, ruling the world:

"Mum, can I start a war?"

"Can I start a war what, dear?"

"Can I start a war, please?"

"Not now. We'll get something on the way back home."

Which, as you know... they will never get. And the world will live in peace... Hopefully.

Notes

BROODING, BRO: THE STORK WISH

1 https://www.abc.net.au/news/2018-03-31/old-toys-prehistoric-society-children-archaeology-anthropology/9493204

HOW TO GET A BUN IN THE OVEN

2 https://www.manchester.ac.uk/discover/news/human-eggs-prefer-some-mens-sperm-over-others-research-shows/

LOOK WHO'S TALKING

3 http://doctoranddad.com/mispronouncing-words-good-kid/

About the Author

A Brazilian journalist, writer and aspiring comedienne who has lived abroad since 2004. Passionate about human's rights, humans and rights, in no particular order. I'm also a mother of two boys, a volunteer doula, an activist for birthing women, a feminist, a former catwalk model, I did singing gigs in restaurants, wrote poetry since I was ten, started learning the piano, the drums and the flamenco, did drama courses, was a ghost in a play and I am a yellow belt in Karate. I did all this because I was told that I couldn't write. As you can see, I can write. The people who told me I couldn't write, didn't say anything about writing well, so the joke is on them.

Also by Andreia Nobre

The Grumpy Guide to Radical Feminism

Tired of explaining reality to fiercely obstinate men about why women need feminism, Journalist and writer Andreia Nobre took the task to clarify some of the misconceptions widely spread about the feminist theory and radical feminism. The author would like to make it very clear that feminists don't hate all men - but you can, if you want to.

The Grumpy Guide to Quit Smoking

It's a "lighter" decision for some. It may all be up in smoke. All puns intended.

Printed in Great Britain
by Amazon